DEATH BLADE

Frost chopped at the rope on his left wrist; the rope frayed, his skin bled from the knife. He pulled; the rope snapped. He hacked apart the rope across his abdomen.

Knives were slicing at him as he leaned forward—nausea, pain, all of it drowning him. He hacked free his right ankle; blood spurted from his skin as the knife blade cut too deep. A sword was chopping down toward him. Frost reached into the crowd of devil-worshipers, snatching at a man by his shoulder-length hair, throwing the body across his own, like a shield.

The sword drove home; the man screamed, his body shuddering. Frost rolled the body away, hacked free his left ankle, then half-rolled, half-fell from the slab to the stone floor!

He felt knives cutting at him, heard the whooshing of swords somehow above the screams and the chanting. He rammed his knife blade forward, into the chest of a man starting to turn toward him, in the man's right hand a sword.

The body lurched back. Frost's right hand lost the knife, but snatched at the sword.

The one-eyed man's right fist balled around the ornately carved hilt and he shouted. "Die!"

THE SURVIVALIST SERIES
by Jerry Ahern

#1: TOTAL WAR   (768, $2.25)

The first in the shocking series that follows the unrelenting search for ex-CIA covert operations officer John Thomas Rourke to locate his missing family—after the button is pressed, the missiles launched and the multimegaton bombs unleashed . . .

#2: THE NIGHTMARE BEGINS   (810, $2.50)

After WW III, the United States is just a memory. But ex-CIA covert operations officer Rourke hasn't forgotten his family. While hiding from the Soviet occupation forces, he adheres to his search!

#3: THE QUEST   (851, $2.50)

Not even a deadly game of intrigue within the Soviet High Command, the formation of the American "resistance" and a highly placed traitor in the new U.S. government can deter Rourke from continuing his desperate search for his family.

#4: THE DOOMSAYER   (893, $2.50)

The most massive earthquake in history is only hours away, and Communist-Cuban troops, Soviet-Cuban rivalry, and a traitor in the inner circle of U.S. II block Rourke's path. But he must go on—he is THE SURVIVALIST.

#5: THE WEB   (1145, $2.50)

Blizzards rage around Rourke as he picks up the trail of his family and is forced to take shelter in a strangely quiet Tennessee valley town. Things seem too normal here, as if no one has heard of the War; but the quiet isn't going to last for long!

#13

THEY CALL ME THE MERCENARY

NAKED BLADE, NAKED GUN

BY AXEL KILGORE

ZEBRA BOOKS
KENSINGTON PUBLISHING CORP.

ZEBRA BOOKS

are published by

KENSINGTON PUBLISHING CORP.
475 Park Avenue South
New York, N.Y. 10016

Printed in the United States of America

For the people who read about Hank Frost—the ones who call, who write, and who count the one-eyed man their late-night friend.

Chapter One

Hank Frost eyed the black-faced Rolex on his left wrist, comparing it to the almost impossibly stylized clock behind the bar. He nodded to himself, murmuring, "What the hell?" then signaled the barman. He had started drinking scotch again and he told the bartender, "Another of the same, friend."

Bess—soon.

He looked at the Rolex again, counting the minutes. Her overseas flight from London to Atlanta would be landing in twenty-four minutes—if the arrival was on time. He glanced past the wall clock, to the television monitor bank—the monitors showed the status of arrivals and departures.

According to the monitor, the flight would be on time.

His drink arrived. Twenty-two minutes to go. He started working on it. His head ached dully, its skin still discolored and sensitive where he had stopped a piece of exploding bridge down in Miami.* And he was a little stiff still from the inactivity the injury had imposed on him.

He smiled, downing the scotch. Seeing Bess would make it all worthwhile. As he felt a twinge of pain near his head wound he revised the idea—not *all* worthwhile.

*See: *They Call Me the Mercenary # 12, Headshot.*

He searched his pockets, finding the half-empty pack of Camels, taking one, then searching his pockets again for the battered Zippo wind lighter. He rolled the striking wheel under his right thumb and poked the tip of the cigarette into the blue-yellow flame—the flame danced in the artificial breeze of the air conditioning.

Frost flicked the cowling closed, dropping the lighter back into an outside pocket of his blue three-piece suit. He'd tried to look presentable for Bess. He tossed money on the bar and the barman nodded as Frost started out, straightening his half-mast black silk crocheted tie, a dozen roses in his left hand. He felt awkward carrying them.

He'd chosen the bar outside the airport security system, despite the fact that he was unarmed; the Metalified High Power and the Gerber knife were locked in the glove compartment of the rental car he had parked in one of the lots. Security systems of any kind made him nervous and airport security systems, however mundane, were no different.

Frost had known of a man in the early days of the systems who had used a pacemaker. When he had passed through the metal detectors, his pacemaker had skipped and stopped and the man had died. And there were always the occasional stray metallic objects that gave the machinery fits as well—his money clip, his lighter. He'd once heard of a Russian tourist being trapped by the machines. The man's teeth had almost all been replaced on the left side of the mouth, and Soviet dentists, at least at that time, had used stainless steel. The Soviet tourist had been searched repeatedly, detained by airport security. Finally a dentist had been called in to verify the construction of the false teeth.

These horror stories, Frost had always secretly felt,

could occur at any time.

He waited in line, dutifully, then walked under the arch.

"Could you please step over there, sir?" the pretty black woman in the security-guard outfit asked.

Frost shrugged, saying, "Sure," then walked the few paces to a male guard who stood beside a small table.

"Would you please empty your pockets, sir?"

"Sure," Frost told him, lighting a cigarette with the Zippo since he had it in his hands. He set down his wallet, his money clip, his change, his hotel room key, the rental car key, and his regular key ring—for the apartment in South Bend that he almost never visited. He set down the roses.

All he left in his pockets was his handkerchief.

The security man used the "wand," running the thing between Frost's legs and against his crotch. Frost asked, "You ever get any guys who tell you that feels good?"

The security guard didn't answer. Buzzing, the wand swept his legs, his arms, his coat.

"I'm getting a reading—"

"My watch," Frost told him, using his thumbnail to pry open the flip-lock clasp of the Rolex's stainless-steel band. He set the watch on the table. "There."

The man wanded him again, this time no electronic whine. "Fine, sir—thank you for your cooperation."

"Right." Frost picked up his belongings, stuffing them into his pockets and resecuring the Rolex. As he closed the clasp on the Rolex's bracelet, he looked at the time, then started to run, murmuring, "Damn it!" Bess's plane would be touching down in eleven minutes.

Running now down the almost ridiculously high and steep moving stairway to reach the lower level, he took the escalator down to the pedestrian walkways. A recorded, robotlike female voice piped over the pedestrian hall speaker system, reminding him that if he wished to travel more than one concourse in distance, he could use the subway.

Frost eyed the moving sidewalk, then heard the wind-rushing sound of a train coming in the subway tunnel to his right. He ran for the train, its doors opening as he reached it.

Frost stepped inside.

A voice, male this time, sounding like a cross between a malevolent machine and an FM announcer, warned that he should stay clear of the doors and hold one of the handrails or take a seat. The doors slammed closed with a pneumatic hiss and slap; the train accelerated rapidly.

Glancing at his watch, Frost stared ahead, into the lighted tunnel. He suddenly realized there was a cigarette, burned out, in the tips of his fingers. He looked for an ashtray.

"Where the hell is—?" Frost stopped, seeing a face at the opposite end of the car. A face he hadn't seen since Vietnam, before he had lost his eye. A face he had sometimes fallen asleep dreaming he'd see again. "Martin!" Frost, feeling his hands trembling with rage, started across the car. "Martin!" he shouted.

People in the small subway car—a blond-haired woman with a little boy in tow, a black man in a three-piece suit who looked as if he was in a hurry, a Hindu woman draped in a sari and carrying a portfolio under her arm—stared at him.

"Martin! You murderous bastard!"

The man at the far rear of the car looked up from the magazine he had seemed to absorb osmotically. "I'm sorry?"

"Vietnam—Major Yates—that deuce-and-a-half

you were driving—Martin!"

"What?"

The man to whom Frost spoke looked up from the magazine, innocently; then his right hand snapped out, the magazine slapping Frost across the right eye. The one-eyed man winced. The subway car, stopping, lurched as a mechanical voice warned everyone to hold on, specified which concourse was coming up, and cautioned passengers to stay clear of the doors.

Martin was up, his left foot snapping out, missing Frost's chin by less than inches as Frost rocked back against the Indian woman. The doors opened; the Indian woman screamed, tugging at the folds of her sari as Frost pushed himself away from her, lurching toward Martin, his hands reaching out, the roses dropping from his left fist. The tips of his fingers touched the shoulders of Martin's jacket as Martin pushed aside the blond-haired woman and her little boy and burst through, out of the car and into the pedestrian mall.

Frost stumbled forward, half-tripping over the woman, helping the little boy up, then shouting. "Martin!" The one-eyed man started to run, away from the now-closing pneumatic doors, across a broad expanse of carpeted corridor—after Martin.

Martin looked back once, while leaping a solid low wall that functioned as a railing for the moving sidewalk to Frost's left as Frost chased him back along the tunnel. The moving sidewalk was going forward; Martin knocked an old woman to her knees as he pushed past her against the flow of traffic.

Frost ran beside the railinglike wall, outdistancing Martin who was running against the moving sidewalk's motion.

Frost was parallel to him now, vaulting the railing, reaching for him.

11

Frost's left hand snaked out, grabbing at the collar of Martin's suit coat, reaching. Frost's fist balled around it now. The one-eyed man threw his weight down, reached with his right hand, grabbed at Martin's right arm, wrestled him down onto the rubber floor of the moving sidewalk.

Martin's left fist lashed back, missing Frost's face by inches. Frost moved his left hand from the collar of Martin's jacket. Grabbing at the side of Martin's head, he snapped it back as he closed his fingers around Martin's right ear.

Martin was on top of him now, and Frost felt an elbow smash into his abdomen. The wind was knocked out of him; his grip on Martin's right ear loosened. Martin shook him away, wheeling, then losing his balance as he tried a kick. Frost dodged the foot, grabbed at it, caught the ankle and pulled, twisting. Martin fell back, half-across the low wall.

Frost was on his feet now, reaching, grabbing Martin by the front of his shirt, by the vest, drawing him up, toward him as the one-eyed man's right fist hammered forward, crossing Martin's jaw. The head snapped back; the body weight sagged for an instant.

Frost stepped in, his right knee smashing up, missing Martin's groin, slamming instead against Martin's left thigh as Martin raised it to guard himself.

Martin's left fist punched forward, catching the one-eyed man in the abdomen, his right arced up, skating off the left side of Frost's jaw as Frost turned his head away.

Frost fell back; Martin started to run again.

In the background, amid the screams, the shouts, the curses, Frost could hear the crackling of a radio.

He looked to his right. A uniformed security guard was reaching for him.

Frost dodged the man, ran along the moving side-

12

walk again, after Martin.

Martin reached the end of the moving sidewalk, Frost after him. A security man tried a flying tackle. Frost dodged it. "Just like football," the one-eyed man rasped as he kept running.

Martin was reaching the escalator now, its steepness again seeming almost ridiculous as Frost watched Martin going up, this time with the flow of traffic. Martin took the stairs in a run, two at a time, knocking people aside like bowling pins.

Frost was behind him, stepping over some people Martin had left in his wake, sliding past others. Martin was halfway up as Frost reached out again, grabbed him by the coattails, jerked him back. Frost fell, Martin on him, rolling over him.

On his knees on the escalator steps, Frost reached out, his left hand grabbing for Martin's face, his left thumb hooking in the right side of Martin's mouth. Martin tried biting, but the pressure wasn't there long enough as Frost ripped at the cheek. Martin screamed; blood spurted outward. Frost's right fist hammered forward, crushing into Martin's mouth and nose. Martin fell back, Frost diving for him as he sprawled upside down on the steps of the escalator.

Frost felt it before he saw it, the foot hammering up into his crotch, the blinding flash of gold and yellow and red in his eye as he fell forward, over Martin's body, sprawling against a woman who screamed.

Frost rolled onto his back, his elbows propped against one of the escalator treads.

Martin was up, running, a handkerchief pressed to the right side of his face where Frost had ripped his cheek.

Frost started to his feet, Martin was off the escalator now, running toward the security arches, Frost behind him.

Frost saw a flash of uniform to his left and felt something hammer hard across his shins; his legs went out from under him.

Frost rolled with it, onto his back, his legs numb, a streak of brown or black snaking down toward him—his head. . . .

Chapter Two

From behind his hands, Frost looked up and heard the security guard say, "He could be dangerous, ma'am."

Bess, brushing her blond hair away from her face with the back of her left hand, smiled, first at Frost, then at the security guard. "I know he's dangerous—that's why I love him."

The security guard smiled, then closed the door.

"Hi, Mommie—got myself in trouble." Frost laughed, standing up.

"I heard," she almost whispered. She looked him up and down. "The handcuffs don't go with the suit."

"Yeah—tried tellin' 'em they clashed." He grinned.

"Hold me." And she came forward. Frost, raising his hands, his wrists cuffed together, encircled her with his arms.

His mouth came down on hers, their tongues touching, Frost feeling the wetness, the warmth of her lips against his. She pulled back, breathing hard. Frost looked into her green eyes. "Hi, kid."

"I love you," she whispered.

"I know—I love you, too," he told her.

"What happened—why—"

Frost raised his arms, Bess stooping as he got his arms from around her. He sat down on the straight-backed orange plastic chair; Bess stood in front of him. She wore a blue suit, the jacket short, her white blouse tied at the neck in a bow. She sat down on the chair beside him then, sweeping her skirt under her, crossing her legs, and slipping her elevated left foot half-out of the dark blue high-heeled shoe she wore. Again she brushed her blond hair—past shoulder length now—back from her face, her eyes studying him.

"This guy Martin—I knew him, from years ago in Vietnam. Didn't really know him—I recognized him. It was before I lost my eye. I was just a first lieutenant then. Anyway—"

The door to the hallway opened. Frost, looking up, stopped in mid-thought. It was the plain-clothes police lieutenant who had taken his story. "Captain Frost," he murmured, then looked at the woman. "Miss—if you'd like to—"

"My name is Bess Stallman. I'm a television reporter—and I'm also this man's fiancèe—what's going on?" Bess got up from the chair, standing bolt upright, her fingers splayed against her thighs as she looked the police officer in the eye, their faces inches apart.

"I was just about," the lieutenant began, producing a long Safariland handcuff key and reaching down to Frost's wrists, "to tell Captain Frost that we checked his story. He's free to go. Checked with Department of Defense, verified his report of the slaying when he was stationed in Saigon. There's no line—at least nothing we've got—on this Martin character."

"It probably isn't his right name. I just saw it for an instant on the fatigue blouse he was wearing then," Frost said.

"Lot of crazy things happened in Vietnam, Frost. I'd say forget it. And if y'all see this Martin guy again, get a cop. Don't take the law into your own hands."

Frost stood up as the police lieutenant loosed the

16

last of the two bracelets. Frost rubbed his wrists. "The airport police have your things I think," the man added. He started for the door. "Sorry we had to detain you," he said, half over his shoulder. "No one's pressing charges for the fight. You're free to go; but if you can, stay around Atlanta, or at least notify me if you leave town, so I can contact you if we get a line on this Martin fella."

Still rubbing his wrists, Frost took the proffered card from the police lieutenant. His head ached badly where the night stick had crashed down on it; his shins hurt where the night stick had rapped them. "You won't get a line on Martin—army intelligence didn't in Vietnam; the MPs never came up with anything."

"Wait and see." The lieutenant shrugged, disappearing into a small hallway, closing the door behind him.

Frost took Bess into his arms for a moment, saying, "Now let's do this properly." Her arms circled his neck, his hands gripped her waist, pulling her closer to him, his mouth found hers. . . .

"What took so long?" It was the security sergeant at the small desk outside the detention room.

Frost looked at Bess, then at the sergeant, who was trying to keep a straight face. "It was the shock of being arrested, I guess."

"Right." The man nodded, then added, "But of course y'all weren't arrested—just detained for questioning."

Frost rubbed his wrists. "Right—after a crack on the head with a night stick. I'd love to see what you call being arrested. Gimme my stuff," Frost snapped, "before I start breaking furniture."

The security sergeant started to his feet; Bess stepped between them. "He was just kidding."

Frost caught the sparkle of the diamond in the tiger's-mouth ring she wore on the third finger of her left hand, and he smiled as he remembered how it had saved her life really.* "Yeah—I'm just kidding," he lied.

Frost replaced his Rolex, rubbing away a smudge on the crystal as he did; then he refilled his pockets. "I need y'all to sign this inventory receipt," the sergeant said.

"What if I don't?" Frost asked.

"He'll sign," Bess insisted.

Frost looked at her, then nodded. "I'll sign. Give it to me."

He signed the receipt. The man, reaching behind him, handed Frost the bouquet of roses; most of the petals were gone. Bess took them from his hands.

The one-eyed man shrugged. "I tried," he told her.

"They were beautiful—I know you tried," she whispered, rising up on her toes and kissing his cheek.

They started from the security section, into the terminal beyond, Frost's right arm going around her waist. He told her, "Come on—buy you a drink— I know I need one."

*See: They Call Me the Mercenary #8 and #9, *Assassin's Express* and *The Terror Contract.*

Chapter Three

"You want scotch?"

"With ice," she told him.

Frost nodded, then looked at the bartender. "Two scotches—on the rocks."

"You want the house brand?"

"Not from around here, are you? I missed the 'y'all' and everything."

"Jersey. What kinda scotch you want?"

"Cutty," Frost answered, taking the first good brand name that came into his head. Unless you got into the very cheap stuff, Frost was of the opinion that scotch was scotch.

"So tell me about Martin," Bess began, taking one of Frost's cigarettes from his pocket. "I shouldn't see you—only time I smoke."

"How come you find 'em so easily—hell, I gotta frisk myself for my cigarettes."

"Give me a light and tell me about Martin," she insisted.

"What the hell is all this commotion about?" Frost gestured beyond the windows of the bar into the terminal itself. "Wall-to-wall people out there and people running around with Bibles—"

"I was on the plane with him."

"Who?" Frost asked. Finally finding his Zippo, he lit her cigarette, then lit one for himself.

"Dr. Lassiter Kulley—he's part of the reason I'm

here. He's the television evangelist—not a member of any special church. I don't even know if the 'Doctor' part is legitimate. But he's popular in Europe, here. I interviewed him on the plane—a good, long one. He's peculiar—but I guess he believes in what he's doing."

"You mean you flew all the way from London to Atlanta to interview a preacher?"

"No—that was just a bonus—the interview. But it's because of him I was coming here," she said, molding a glowing tip out of the ashes of her cigarette.

"I'm not following you—"

"Your head—is it—"

"Yeah—that's an old wound." Frost smiled, gesturing toward the discolored spot near his hairline on the left side. "The new bump's up here." He pointed to the top of his head. "Ouch," he exclaimed as she reached out and touched it.

"Frost—can't leave you alone for—"

"Tell me about Kelly."

"It's Kulley—with a *U* and an *E*. Not much to tell, really—but I'm here to work up background stuff for a series the bureau's doing about satanic cultists and ritual mutilation murders—not just in the U.S., but in Europe, too. There've been a couple around here and I figured it was a good excuse to—"

"Yeah." Frost smiled. "I'm glad you did. Saved me the airfare to London."

"Turkey," she murmured.

"What's this Kulley guy got to do with it?"

"He speaks out against satanic cults periodically in his sermons—just did a series of sermons about them on his European evangelistic tour. He says they're a serious threat, cause thousands of murders each year, and are part of a demonic conspiracy aimed at taking over the minds of Christian youth."

"Sent a Jewish reporter to help save Christian youth

20

from the devil?"

"Something like that." She smiled. "Should be a good story. I'll work up the research; then local film crews will get the tapes I need worked up. We'll dub and we'll have a series for some of the news programs we feed."

"And I always thought the filming and the narration took place at the same time."

"Sure." She smiled. "Anyway—wanna help me scout out devil-worshipers?"

"If it's the way to spend the most time with you, then yeah—I'll help you scout up devil-worshipers. But it's a pile of crap."

"Well—probably just a lot of people who like to play at being witches and a few genuine crazies who like to kill."

"What are the killings like?"

"Usually teenage girls—runaways. Probably hitchhikers, picked up then killed. Designs are sometimes carved on their bodies, sometimes they're painted with goat's blood—"

"Goat's blood?" Frost asked.

"No—ya ordered scotch," the barman said, bringing the drinks. Frost looked across at the man, but the man was already turning away.

"Goat's blood," Bess reiterated. "Usually been stabbed in the abdomen, sometimes some of the internal organs—"

"Aww—that's . . ." Frost downed half his glass of scotch.

"What—weak stomach?"

"Yeah—for stuff like that," Frost told her.

"Still gonna help me?" she asked, her voice soft. She exhaled smoke through her nostrils as she stubbed out her cigarette.

"Yeah—can't let you go after wackos like that your-

21

self. Yeah." Frost lit another cigarette, with the tip of the burned-down butt in his fingers.

"Tell me about Martin, now," she asked again.

"Well—like I started to say back there in security. I don't know the guy. I saw his face, read a nametag on his fatigue blouse. He was driving a deuce-and-a-half that—"

"Deuce-and-a-half," she interrupted. "That's a two-and-one-half-ton truck—right?"

"You're gettin' good, kid." Frost smiled. "But he was driving this thing anyway, and he ran over Maj. Clevon Yates—my C.O. for a while when I was detached to G-2 in Saigon. Hell of a good guy, and a good friend. Truck ran him over—squashed his head like a—"

"Frost!" Bess cautioned, her shoulders shivering.

"Well—he was dead anyway. I tried running down the truck—guy whipped me off the hood of the truck though when he made a fast turn with it. I told G-2, told the MPs, swore out papers for this Martin. They all told me the same thing. There was no Martin with access to a deuce-and-a-half at that time of the day and no Martin that matched the guy's face. And there was too much mud on the truck for me to give them any numbers anyway. I always figured it was some kind of intelligence job and they just didn't want to let me in on it. But anyway—I saw him today on the way to meet you. I was so damned hot to get him I didn't use my head—angry, you know." Frost inhaled hard on the cigarette.

"I know," she reassured him. "Do you want to—?" She gestured with her head toward the door, not finishing the question.

Frost smiled, downing most of the rest of his drink. "Yeah—let's split."

He put the money for the tab and a tip on the bar,

22

stood up, and helped her down from the barstool. "If you wouldn't wear tight skirts, you wouldn't have trouble with barstools."

She smiled at him, saying, "That's why women wear straight skirts—so men can help them down from barstools, Frost—hmm?"

He gently patted her rear end as he put his right arm around her. . . .

They spoke more of Kulley on the way to the hotel, Frost having retrieved his weapons from the glove compartment, then threaded his way onto the interstate. "Why do you keep moving left?" she asked him once.

"In Atlanta, they keep canceling out the right-hand lanes—all of a sudden, wham. 'Right Lane Must Exit'—you know." He dodged left one lane then, realizing as he crossed through downtown Atlanta that the left lane was vanishing too, feeding off. Both hands locked on the steering wheel as he passed the entrances with no acceleration ramps; he turned off on the Interstate 285 by-pass around the city.

"You're going to Chattanooga?"

"No—but if I wanted to, this is the—"

"Ohh," she murmured. "Do you know what you're doing, Frost?"

"Look," he told her, "I memorized the route from the hotel to the airport and I'm—"

"You're following it back—just like a rat gets out of a maze," she finished. "That's a sound procedure."

"I'm glad to see our absence from one another didn't soften you up," Frost cracked. "This Kulley guy—think he's right? Demonic conspiracies and everything?"

"I hope he isn't," she answered.

They both fell silent after that, Frost turning off the expressway, onto an access road, then up a steep hill

23

and down to the hotel. As he turned into the parking lot, Bess murmured, "We've almost made it."

"Cut the cracks," he told her good-naturedly. Sliding into a space, he put the rented Ford's selector into "Park," then applied the emergency brake. He shut off the motor and got out. As he opened Bess's door, she said, "Before we go in—wanna walk a little?"

"Over there—where it's green?" he asked her.

"Uh-huh—I wanna talk—about us."

"O.K." The one-eyed man lit a cigarette as he started to walk beside her.

It wasn't a park, just a green expanse, where no buildings stood, across the road from the parking lot. Frost and Bess dodged the traffic to get there, then slowed to a walk.

"I've got one thing I want to say," she finally told him, turning around, looking up at him.

"And what is it?" he asked her.

"I know marriage scares you—so let's live in sin, until then." Frost folded her into his arms, holding her. They said nothing for a long time. Eventually, still silent, they sat on the grass. Frost didn't know what to say to her.

After a long time—his pack of cigarettes was nearly empty—they walked back across to the parking lot, got her luggage from the trunk of his rented car, and brought it inside. A bellman carried it to the elevators, on which Frost and Bess rode up with him to Frost's floor. Frost tipped him as he deposited the luggage.

As the bellman closed the door, Bess turned, looking at Frost. Frost, without walking toward her, said, "Once you're done with this—and it's not an excuse—this—this story of yours that you're doing. Once you're done with it, then let's talk—plan. You're right—I am scared of it—marriage. But I think I'm more scared of losing you."

She ran into his arms, Frost holding her tightly against him. . . .

They lay beside one another, their hands exploring each other's bodies. She rested her head on his left shoulder, his right hand lay against her left breast. She leaned up, kissing his chin. The one-eyed man took her face in his hands, kissing her eyelids, her lips, her neck. He leaned over her, his left hand under her, holding her half in his arms, the fingers of his right hand tracing across her abdomen.

He could feel her hands on him, rubbing him, making his body more aware of hers with each second, each motion as he slid between her thighs. He explored her with his hands, her body moving under him, her lips touching his chest, his neck, his face; she moaned his name—"Frost." He bent over her, kissing her, his mouth crushing hers, feeling her hands again as he came inside of her. Her body moved, trembled, seemed to him to breathe with his. It lasted a long time for them, he knew; but not long enough. . . .

Frost sat on the edge of the bed. "Come on—get a shower, then buy me dinner," Bess said.

"I don't need a shower," he answered.

Wearing one of his shirts, Bess, her suitcases as yet unpacked, stepped into the bathroom doorway. "Can I tell ya the truth?"

"Yeah," he told her. "Yeah."

"You need a shower."

Frost shrugged. "O.K.—I'll take the hint. Don't need a brick wall to fall on—"

"Anyway," she interrupted, "we have someplace we have to go tonight."

"We already did that," he said straight-faced, dodging as she came at him and swung. "Just kid-

25

ding." He laughed, pushing a chair between her and himself.

"Well, I'm not. We've got a date tonight."

"What?"

"My story—with Dr. Julian Wells."

"Who's he?"

"He's an expert in the occult. My bureau arranged for us to meet—and guess what we're going to do!"

Frost looked at Bess and laughed. She reminded him of a little girl—especially wearing his shirt which was vastly big on her. "I don't like guessing games."

She came into his arms, murmuring, "I could make you."

Frost nodded. "O.K.—so I can't guess—what?"

"A black mass."

The one-eyed man sat back on the edge of the bed. Bess stared down at him. "Aww," he groaned.

Chapter Four

Frost edged the rented car into a parking spot between a rifle rack equipped pickup truck—an umbrella and a level rode where the rifles should have been—and a Volkswagen Beetle. "You have any idea where we are?" she asked him.

"Sure—about a half-block from Wells's house. See—I studied a map."

"I'll believe we're a half-block from his house when I see the house."

"Faithless person," he murmured, sliding out and locking his door, then coming around behind the car and getting her out on the curb side. "Wells's house should be—holy shit—"

"Frost?"

"Look." Frost pointed toward the far end of the block, at a tall, perhaps three-story-high frame structure.

"That's his house—I remember it from one of his books." Bess gasped.

"Get the fire department and the cops—hurry!" Frost started to run. The upper story of the house, either an attic or a full third floor—he couldn't tell which—was in flames. That feeling he'd had in the car as they'd driven over, the idea of going to a witches' service—it had given him the creeps. And now a fire. Frost skidded on his heels as he reached the storybook-looking white picket fence surrounding the old

27

Victorian house. Ignoring the gate over the sidewalk. Frost jumped the railing, half-stumbling as he came down on a tree root, and he lurched ahead across the manicured yard, running toward the house.

The flames were leaping higher now; the entire rear portion of the third floor or attic was ablaze.

The low porch seemed to surround the house rather than front it. Frost took the front steps in one long leap.

He opened the screen door. The front door—he tried the knob—was locked.

He looked behind him into the street, then reached under his jacket, snatching the Metalifed Browning High Power from its Cobra Comvest shoulder rig and whacking the butt of the pistol against the glass in the door. The glass shattered in huge chunks, falling inward. He reached his left hand inside, found the latch on the plate-type lock, worked it, then twisted the knob and pushed the door inward; the screen slammed against him from behind.

He rammed the pistol into the waistband of his pants, under his vest, and started toward the steps at the far end of the hallway. Smoke was filtering down from the upper level, a crackling popcornlike sound filled the air as well—the roof going, perhaps the walls catching?

Frost took the steps two at a time, toward the landing above. The smoke was thicker above him, but he raced up the second flight, to the second floor. The smoke was thick here; his eye watered, his breathing was labored, his throat burned. He coughed, doubling over with the spasm.

There was a scream then—a man's scream, heavy, loud, almost in itself incorporating shame for existing as a scream.

Frost looked around the top floor, the smoke thick,

so thick he couldn't see clearly for any great distance. He dropped to his knees, peered under the smoke cloud, and at the far end of the second floor, saw an open doorway. Bright orange light flickered near it. He heard the scream again; this time he placed the sound.

Inhaling deeply of the fresher air near the floor, the one-eyed man forced himself to his feet and stormed toward the open doorway at the far end of the floor. He half-collapsed beside it, the walls hot as the bare skin of his hands touched them. He turned, facing the doorway, and dropping to his knees to breathe, looked up a narrow hallway. Shallow, winding steps led upward. An attic. And he heard the scream again.

Frost inhaled. Forcing himself to his feet, he started up the stairs, toward the flames and the origin of the scream.

His eye tearing so heavily it was hard to see, he tripped, his hands splaying out on the staircase before him, a strange sound above him. Shaking his head to clear it, he looked up. There was a knife, slicing the air and cutting down toward his throat.

Frost pushed himself up, back; the knife flashed past him. His hands reached out into the smoke seeking the black sleeve to which the knife seemed attached. He found the arm, twisted it. The knife fell as Frost, trying to bring his attacker in view below the smoke, tugged at the arm.

A black hood, a black monster face beneath it, a robe covering the body.

Frost punched his right fist into the middle of the face—the monster face was a gas mask.

The one-eyed man ripped the mask away with his left hand, the High Power in his right, the pistol arcing downward. Frost split the bridge of the nose wide with it, laying open the middle of the forehead as

29

well. He hammered the gun down again, the butt this time against the base of the nose. The tear-streaming eyes of the man who had worn the gas mask stared, open wide—dead.

Frost pulled the GI gas mask over his own face, popping its cheeks as he blew out to form a seal and inhaled deeply, tasting the stale, filtered air, noxious-smelling—but good to breathe.

Frost pushed himself to his feet, started up the stairs again.

Ahead of him, over the crackling of the flames, the sagging sounds of timbers, he heard footsteps. The gas mask he wore protected his right eye, but because of the density of the smoke, he could see only a few feet ahead of him. The Browning in his right fist, he kept going, hugging the wall for secure footing despite the heat emanating from it.

He stopped dead. Two black, spectral shapes came toward him, hooded, robed, like the man he had killed near the base of the steps. Frost edged back, closer to the wall, the pistol in his right fist cocked, the safety wiping down under his thumb. He shouted through the mask. "Get the hell out of my way!"

The nearer of the two figures hurtled himself toward Frost, down the stairs. The one-eyed man fired his pistol, point-blank, twice, into the figure's center of mass. The body thudded against him. Frost discharged the pistol twice more to punch the body back and away; it rolled toward the railing, tumbling over it into the pit of smoke near the base of the stairwell. Frost wheeled, losing his balance. The High Power slipped from his fingers, clattering to the steps below him. The second robed figure was coming, a long, curved-bladed knife in its gloved right hand.

Frost reached to the small of his back, pushing himself to his feet as he did; the tiny Gerber Mk-I boot knife was now tight in his right fist. "Come on, sucker," the one-eyed man snapped through the mask he wore.

The hooded figure edged back, then lunged forward. Frost swiped at the knife hand as it darted over him, then fell back again against the wall. He felt something by his feet, heard it clatter downward—his pistol.

The hooded figure recovered, prepared for another lunge, and behind him was another identically dressed figure, with a knife, larger than the one the first man carried, in his right hand. Frost dropped lower, into a crouch, to get below the smoke a little as the nearer of the two robed figures lunged.

Frost caught the knife arm of his opponent under his own left arm, driving the knife in his fist downward, gouging the inside of the man's elbow, raking the knife toward him, cutting every tendon, muscle, and vein he could manage, then letting go of the arm as the knife clattered away. The one-eyed man's right knee snapped up, smashing into the groin of his attacker; the figure doubled over. Frost punched the spear point of his little knife down into the exposed neck where the hood had pulled away from the robe; the body stiffened under him, fell away. Lunging like a swordsman, the second knife-wielding robed figure was coming for him. Frost back-stepped, falling, skidding down the stairs. The robed attacker lost his balance on the steps, recovered, and started down, his knife punching downward like a dagger. Frost, feeling along the steps for a purchase with his left hand, contacted the familiar outline of the Browning High Power.

He picked up the gun, punching it forward through the smoke, firing, firing, firing again and again as the body of the robed killer twitched and lurched and

31

spun, then tumbled over the railing and down into the smoke.

Frost climbed to his feet, his back against the wall. The wall was hotter to the touch now. He holstered the little Gerber knife, transferred the High Power to his right fist, and started up the stairs again.

He reached the landing. Ahead of him was a narrow hallway, and at its end a glowing light. "Fire," he rasped through the mask. The one-eyed man started forward, toward the small room at the end of the hall. He held the pistol cocked and ready in his right hand, close to his body so it couldn't be swatted away in a surprise attack.

He stopped, in the doorframe of the small room at the end of the hall.

Bess had shown him a picture, from the dust jacket of a book. The face he saw—upside down—was that of Julian Wells, the expert on the occult. The head was where the feet should be, a bizarre symbol, carved, bloody, in the center of his forehead. Wells was screaming; blood dribbled from the corners of his mouth and ran down into his nose.

Wells's arms were outstretched at his sides, the palms outward, nailed into the wall, his legs stretched upward, the feet bound together with cord, a nail driven through the insteps into the wall. And the front of Wells's body—the shirt and vest ripped away—was painted in red like blood.

Frost, fighting to control his desire to vomit, shuddered and leaned against the door frame. Then he started forward, ramming the pistol into his belt. As he reached Julian Wells, something cracked behind him and Frost turned; a long-bladed knife—a sword?—chopped downward. Frost hurtled himself back, his body falling against Wells's body as the robed figure who held the blade—it was a sword—

32

started toward him.

"You suckers don't give up," Frost snapped. He started to reach for his gun, but couldn't, dodging instead as the sword arced out toward him in some movement of a martial art–like cata.

The sword was spinning, arcing, almost a living thing in the hands of the hooded, robed figure who wielded it. Frost, snatching up a wooden chair, blocked a sword cut. The chair splintered under the impact of the blade as Frost dropped to his knees and threw himself across the floor.

The sword was slicing downward again; Frost, finally having the Browning in his right hand, was firing. The figure stood, motionless, sword poised for the cut, as Frost pumped the trigger of his pistol. The slide of the High Power locked open, the last of the 115-grain JHPs fired. The robed swordsman seemed to shudder, once, then fell to his knees and was still.

Unsteadily, Frost got to his feet, extracted the High Power's spent magazine, and dropped the empty into a side pocket of his suit. He could see where the suit was ripped and torn—ruined. He rammed a fresh thirteen-round magazine up the butt of the pistol and worked the slide stop downward; the slide rammed forward. He scanned the smoke-filled room again, then upped the safety on the pistol, ramming it into his belt. He started toward Julian Wells, trying to determine how to free the injured man from the nails which impaled him to the wall.

On the littered and obviously searched desk at the center of the room was a large, heavy-looking letter opener. Frost snatched it up, then dropped it. He picked up the sword instead, from the hand of the dead killer. It was single-edged, with a short, curving false edge above—its shape like that of an exaggerated Bowie knife. Near its hilt was a gutting hook. Frost

33

approached the injured Wells. "I'm gonna try and get you down, sir—then out of here," Frost told him. "I'm a friend. I know this will hurt."

Frost edged the gutting hook around the nail driven through Wells's feet, then began to pry. There was a bloodcurdling scream and Frost could feel Wells's body shudder. Frost continued to pry; the nail started to come. He pried with all his strength; the nail came free of the wood but was still in Wells's feet. The feet and legs sagged. Frost trembled, sickened, then wedged his own body against Wells to keep the added weight from ripping the flesh of his hands where the nails penetrated. He pried the nail from the feet, blood spurting up toward his gas-masked face. Frost dropped the rusted nail to the floor of the burning, smoky room, then used the edge of the sword to cut the rope around the ankles.

His back against Wells now, Frost worked at prying loose the nail in his right hand. He had it; the nail came out of the wood and the hand at once.

"One more," the one-eyed man rasped, prying now at the nail in the left hand.

The nail came free of the wood; Frost plucked it from the palm of the hand.

He dropped the sword, the steel clattering against the floor; then he turned awkwardly, getting Dr. Wells into his arms, easing the man down from the wall. The man—perhaps in his sixties—seemed half-conscious, but his eyes streamed tears that were more than just the result of the smoke. Turning, staring out through the doorway into the hallway, Frost hugged the frail body to him. The hallway was blocked by a wall of apparently solid flame.

Frost turned toward the far wall—a window there, large, partially open. Frost carried Wells across the room, stopping beside the window and setting Wells down on a couch near it. He tried raising the window higher—it wouldn't budge. Frost tried again. No movement.

He peered through it. Beneath the window sill, perhaps three feet down, was a narrow ledge of roof, some of the roofing material peeling and curling up, possibly the wood beneath rotted.

Frost looked behind him again. Now the doorway was consumed with flames.

Frost picked up a small wooden chair and crashed it against the glass of the window; the glass burst outward. He used the chair again to rake the shards of glass from the frame, then he dropped it. With the bottom of the window where it was, it still barred the full access he needed. Frost half-wheeled, his left foot snapping out in a fast, double kick against the window; the wood splintered, breaking under the impact.

Frost turned to it, inspected it quickly, then wheeled, kicking again, knocking out what remained on the right-hand side of the window.

Frost pulled free the rest, tossing it back into the room, then turned to Dr. Wells. As gently as he could, he raised Wells into a fireman's carry—the thought amused the one-eyed man for a moment. What he needed now more than anything were firemen. Wells across his shoulder, Frost turned to the window. He got his left leg up and out, but his trouser leg caught on a piece of wood. The material ripped as he moved his leg. He straddled the window sill, touching the roof with his left foot, looking for a purchase, a solid footing. Then Frost crouched, easing his body and Dr. Wells's body, which was across his right shoulder, through the opening.

Frost reached for the window sill, almost losing his footing on the roof shingles as he settled his right foot. Below him was a drop of perhaps thirty-five feet, a

35

concrete driveway running its course along the ground to his left. "Shit," Frost murmured, edging along the roof now.

He heard a loud, popping sound, a crackling. He looked to his right; the flames had burst through the front of the roof now and licked upward into the night sky.

Frost started to his left; below him was the concrete driveway that would smash his body were he to fall.

In the distance, he could hear sirens—the fire department? He silently prayed for it.

He loosed the grip of his right hand along the roof line and ripped the mask away from his face. The air was cold against his sweating skin; its freshness made his head swim. He shook his head, breathed more shallowly. The flames now probed out the window through which he had come, advancing after him, faster than he himself could have moved, and with Wells across his shoulder his own agility was cut.

The sirens were louder now. As Frost looked below him, the view momentarily dizzied him.

He kept moving. The flames were on the roof now, the wind blowing their heat toward him as he dropped the gas mask. It bounced once and lay on the paving of the driveway like a dead, contorted face.

Frost edged along the roof, the burden of Wells's body telling on his own. He moved his right foot forward; it sank as the roofing beneath him gave way. Frost slipped down, catching his balance, his ankle pinned; only his left hand leaning against the roof itself supported him.

He settled back against the roof, supporting his own weight and the weight of Dr. Wells, trying to wrestle his ankle free of the wood. "Kiss off another pair of sixty-five-dollar shoes," he cursed, tugging his foot free; the shoe stuck.

He tried rising to his feet again, but the roof below him was suddenly scorchingly hot. The one-eyed man realized that flames would burst through at any instant. Below him on the street, he could hear the fire trucks stopping, hear the shouts, hear more sirens.

But the noise and commotion were from the front of the house, and he was now at the side. Frost reached for his Metalifed High Power, fired the pistol three times into the air, then waited. Georgia was a state of sportsmen, hunters—and three shots were the universally acknowledged woodsmen's distress signal. Frost fired the pistol again, three shots in rapid succession.

He heard a shout from below him and looked down. "You on the roof!"

If Frost had been Catholic, he would have crossed himself.

Frost limped down the hospital hallway, his ankle didn't hurt, but he was minus a shoe. "The hell with it," he rasped, bending down and taking off the other shoe. There was a trash container a few feet ahead, and he put the shoe in it.

Bess was running toward him from the end of the hallway; a woman walked behind her.

"Frost!" Bess whispered, folding her arms around him.

"I'm all right, kid." He smiled. "Just grubby and shoeless."

"Thank God," she murmured. "I saw the flames, saw—"

"I know," he told her. "Good thing those drunken painters came along when they did."

"Drunken painters?"

"Knew a guy—named Jack. Best friend I ever had. Used to always call firemen that because they ran around frantically with ladders—like drunken painters, you know."

She leaned up and kissed him.

"Captain Frost?"

Frost looked across Bess's shoulder. The woman who had walked behind Bess had spoken.

"Yes," he said, tired, not wanting to talk to anyone really.

Bess said, "This is Blanche Corrigan, Frost—Dr. Wells's secretary."

Frost forced a smile, asking, "How is he? The police—when they were questioning me about those wackos with the knives and swords—they said they didn't know."

"He could live or die—the doctor told me."

"Nothing like hedging your bets," Frost cracked.

"It's so many things." Blanche Corrigan almost sighed. Her hair was a lighter blond color than Bess's, her eyes brown, her build a little on what Frost considered the chunky side. She wore a pair of blue jeans, a purple floral-print blouse outside the waist, and green shoes. The one-eyed man guessed she had dressed in a hurry. "It's smoke inhalation, so much loss of blood—shock. He wasn't the strongest man to begin with, and he's sixty-seven."

"He looked younger," Frost told her.

"He would have liked to hear you say that. He was always vain about his age." She started to cry, sniffed loudly, then looked up from the balled-up tissue in her hands, forcing a smile. "The clock there says almost ten-thirty and that black mass wasn't until midnight—he would have liked me to take you since he can't. Julian—Dr. Wells—he always lived up to his commitments. And he would have wanted me—"

"Hey," Frost told her, taking her hands in his. "This has gotta be—"

"No—it'll be something to do—please. If you feel

38

up to it and the police are through questioning you—please—"

"The cops told me to stay around town. I've got a concealed-weapons permit so there wasn't a problem about the gun."

"Let's do it, Frost," Bess urged.

"All right." The one-eyed man nodded.

"I can pick you both up at your hotel—if you'll tell me where. You'll want to—"

"Yeah." Frost looked at his torn, smoke-dirtied suit and his bare feet. "To change—yeah. O.K." He gave her the name of the hotel and she said she had been there, then walked away, agreeing to meet them in an hour.

As Frost and Bess started to walk from the hospital, Bess told him, "That hole in your right sock. You wouldn't have that if we were married."

"What?" he asked her, lighting a cigarette and almost choking on the smoke. "You darn socks?"

"I don't even darn socks—I'd just buy you a new pair."

Frost held her close, just shaking his head.

Chapter Five

Frost stood under the shower, the hot water streaming down on him. He glanced at the Rolex—it was ten after eleven.

"Hurry up, Frost," Bess called out.

"I will," he answered. Then he could hear her, in the bathroom. He heard the toilet seat lid being raised and imagined what she was going to do.

"Tell me about them—the men who tried—"

"You always interview people while you're urinating?" he called out.

"No—only special like you. Tell me about them."

"All of them wore gas masks—I guess for the fire. Seemed like amateurs—the way they had the fire roaring along and were still inside. Pros wouldn't have done that. And then that guy who threw himself at me down the steps. He had to know I was gonna shoot him. Didn't care." Frost rinsed the shampoo from his hair under the water. "Didn't care."

"What?" she asked. "Talk louder."

"They didn't care," he said again, raising his voice, letting the water stream down his body. "Like fanatics—you know. Die for the cause, that sort of thing."

"Maybe they were Satanists and this isn't some kind of—"

"Maybe," Frost said soberly. "These people to-night—"

"Ohh—they're just witches. It's just to get the feel

40

of the thing. They aren't Satanists. They worship the elements of nature—it's what they call the 'old religion.' If they've got magic, it's white magic.''

"And the Satanists are the black-magic people?" Frost asked her.

"I guess so—if there's any magic at all." He heard the toilet lid going down, and heard the flush. "They may really be blood cultists."

"Awful damned peculiar them trying to kill Wells just when you were going to see him," Frost remarked, turning the water to straight cold, soaking under it.

"Maybe not—could have been something in his research, maybe something else. If they were fanatics like you say, it could have been anything."

"Yeah—but swords in the twentieth century—they gotta be—''

"Why?" she interrupted. "If the death and the ritual are tied together, that may all be a part of what they do."

"What about that symbol they carved into Wells's forehead?"

"It's a pentagram," she called back, her voice farther away. He imagined she was brushing her hair now.

"A pentagram," he repeated. He remembered the five-pointed star. "Hmm—so that's a pentagram." He nodded. He'd always been poor at identifying geometric figures.

Chapter Six

"All right—stick 'em up!"

Reaching under his coat for the High Power, Frost started to push Bess away. The voice from the darkness in Blanche Corrigan's back seat called out, "Bang—you're dead."

"Aww—O'Hara," the one-eyed man snapped.

And then the dome light came on as Blanche Corrigan opened her car door. She stepped out onto the curb near the hotel main entrance, and the man in the back seat did the same. "Frost—just as slow on the draw as ever—gotta practice." O'Hara grinned, extending his hand.

Frost took it, then feigned a punch; the lanky FBI man dodged, laughing. "Good to see you guys."

"It's good to see you, Mike," Bess said warmly, going into O'Hara's arms, kissing him on the cheek and hugging him.

"Hey—watch it." Frost laughed.

"Right—break," O'Hara said, stepping back. "Looks like anytime there's trouble lately, I find you right in the middle of it, Frost. Told any good eye-patch jokes lately, sport?"

"Been kinda busy." Frost nodded. "No—nothing you'd like."

"Well—been kinda busy myself, trackin' down terrorists and Commies and everything—heard the rest of the details about that Florida job you were on. You

shoved it right up old Fidel's bazoo, didn't ya?"
O'Hara laughed.*

"Yeah." Frost laughed. "They hadda get that thing
out with a corkscrew—shoved it in so tight."

Bess coughed, too loudly, and Frost felt her kick
him gently in the left ankle. He looked at her, then at
Blanche Corrigan. Blanche Corrigan looked embar-
rassed. "You all know one another?"

"Yeah—boy do we—" O'Hara laughed.

"We met in Canada—awhile ago, worked together
a few times since," Frost told her.**

"Frost and Agent O'Hara are great friends," Bess
added.

"Most of the time, anyway," Frost said, lighting a
cigarette. "What the hell are you doing here?"

O'Hara looked around him, then, dropping his
voice, said, "Well—see, Dr. Wells contacted the bureau the other day. Said he had some dope on some
kinda terrorist conspiracy. Wanted to tell us about it,
but we shouldn't come to his place. He was supposed
to see us tomorrow morning. I flew down from Washington just to see him. It was on the news about what
happened, so I contacted Miss Corrigan here and she
said the three of you were going out to do some kinda
research."

"Yeah—a black mass," Frost told him.

"A what?"

"A black mass, Mike," Bess repeated.

"What's—what's a black mess, huh?"

"A black mass—it's—is ahh—much like a—
ahh . . ." Frost shrugged.

"It's a service, a convocation of the old religion, the
religion of all our ancestors thousands of years ago and

*See: They Call Me the Mercenary #12, *Headshot*.
**See: They Call Me the Mercenary #5, *Canadian Killing Ground*.

43

in some areas up until long after the dawning of Christianity," Blanche Corrigan explained. "It's a worshiping of the natural forces—"

"So we're gonna see some folks kissin' trees and everything?" O'Hara laughed.

"Mike!" Bess said in a coarse stage whisper.

"Well—I mean, no disrespect or anything, but a black mass? Forces of—"

"The natural forces of the elements, the healing, the feeling—you'll, you'll see. You'll understand. Dr. Wells has taken me to so many of them over the years."

"He was a tree-worshiper?" O'Hara asked, sounding sincere as Frost laughed.

"O'Hara—cut it out. They don't kiss trees," Frost declared. Then he looked at Bess. "Do they?"

"Shut up." She smiled.

The drive took them well out of the city, the houses quickly giving way to woods, the woods dark, like living, lurking shadows. With the windows of the car slightly opened as the car slowed, turning off from the secondary road along which it had been moving, Frost could hear the sounds of crickets and night birds. "Wonderful," he whispered to Bess, sitting in the dark of the back seat beside him. She squeezed his hand, saying nothing.

"Hey Bess?" O'Hara asked from the front seat.

"What, Mike?"

"You said you were doing a story on this satanic stuff—they for real, ya think?"

"I think some of them are, whether it's just that they take themselves for real or it's something more than that."

"Those jokers tonight were for real," Frost interrupted. "Knives and swords and fires—they were for real, all right."

44

"You oughta get rid of that dinky 9mm you carry and get a real gun, Frost—I keep tellin' ya that. Like my .29—now you shoot somebody with that and he's—"

"Please!" Blanche Corrigan asked. "I don't mean to—but could we talk about something else besides killing?"

"Sure," O'Hara said to her. "Sure." He cleared his throat, as if searching for something to say, then, "Ahh—how much longer until we get to the black-mass place?"

"Not much longer at all now. We're running a little late. Look." She pointed toward the edge of the head-lights off to the right.

Frost looked there, seeing perhaps three dozen cars, from junker station wagons to expensive European vehicles—one car was either a Rolls-Royce or a Bent-ley. He couldn't see the hood ornament to tell the dif-ference.

"A lot of people have found real meaning with these rites," Blanche Corrigan explained, turning the car up a dirt road toward the parking area. "And to them it's very important."

"A lot of people from different walks of life, too—judging by the cars," Bess noted.

"I figured this'd be somethin' for rich flakes," O'Hara interjected.

"No—I think it's part of something much bigger," Blanche Corrigan said. "I think . . ." She turned the car into a space between a pickup truck and a Mer-cedes Benz, then cut the lights. "I think it's part of a more general trend in our society. To return to the past, past values, both spiritual and material. And these people have chosen one route. There are many," she concluded.

Having killed the engine, she started out of the car,

but O'Hara said, "Let me get your door, Miss Corrigan."

"Blanche—please," she said, her face not visible because of the darkness.

"Blanche," O'Hara repeated.

Frost, already getting out, started to go around for Bess's door. "I'll slide out this way," she said, coming across the seat. As she stood up, she straightened the back of her skirt. "Wrap skirts unwrap when you—"

She sucked in her breath; Frost wheeled around. A man was standing behind him, holding a torch, his head hooded and a black robe draping his body. The eyes, glowing in the torchlight, seemed to smile as he looked past Frost. "Good evening, Miss Corrigan—friends of yours?"

"Yes—is that you, Harold?"

"Yes—we were all sorry to hear about the fire at Dr. Wells's home. There is hope he'll recover, isn't there?"

"Yes—but slim hope, Harold. This is Mr. O'Hara —he's with the—"

"Department of Interior—special project on cultural phenomenons," O'Hara's voice came back.

"I'm Hank Frost," Frost said, extending his hand; Harold switched the torch and took it. "And the young lady with me is Bess Stallman."

"Ahh—you're the reporter—television?"

"Yes." Bess smiled. "But I'm afraid I'm just doing research now—no cameras."

"Dr. Wells told us he would be bringing you this evening. It's a genuine pleasure. Please—if you'll all follow me, the service is about to begin and—watch your steps—the path is a little tricky."

Harold started off slowly, Frost hanging back to let Blanche Corrigan and O'Hara pass. As O'Hara came within earshot, Frost whispered, "Phenomena—not

46

phenomenons."

O'Hara looked over his shoulder, rasping, "Well—what the hell? Guys in Interior don't speak too good English anyway."

"Ohh." Frost sighed, shaking his head. Bess holding his right hand, Frost started after O'Hara, Blanche Corrigan, and the torch-bearer—Harold. He switched sides with Bess, taking her right hand in his left so his own right hand would be free to grab the High Power.

"Relax," she whispered to him, so Harold wouldn't hear, apparently.

"I am relaxed," Frost told her quietly, helping her up the path, his right fist balling open and shut. "Very relaxed—you wouldn't believe how relaxed I am. If I told you—"

"All right." She laughed. "I believe you're relaxed."

"No, you don't—neither do I," he answered.

At the head of the path, the ground leveled off and through a stand of wide-apart Georgia pines—Frost smiled at the thought: what other kind of pines would you have in Georgia—he could see a fire burning, a bonfire. And in the flickering yellow light of the fire he could see silhouettes of more robed figures, some holding torches, some just holding hands.

"Changing your mind about these people?" Bess asked him.

"Maybe—Harold seems O.K.—but then you never put your worst face forward. We'll see," he told her.

Frost, Bess, O'Hara, and Blanche Corrigan followed Harold to the edge of the clearing. They were still standing in the trees, the nearest portion of the ring of black-robed cultists less than a dozen yards away. "I'm not puttin' ya on," Frost said to Harold. "But, anything I ever read . . . I thought you guys

47

had your religious services—well—"

"Naked?" Harold asked.

"Yeah." Frost nodded, lighting a cigarette.

"We do—usually. But, if we have visitors—well, let me ask you something? Would you want to run around naked in front of a bunch of strangers?"

"Depends on who the— Just kidding." Frost laughed. "No—guess I wouldn't."

"And that's why we wear the robes," Harold explained patiently.

"Is there anything we should—" Bess started.

"Do? Not really. I'm sorry we don't have folding chairs or anything for seats. Just make yourselves comfortable and if you have any questions afterward, I'll be happy to explain as well as I can. And if I can't handle it, we can ask the priestess."

"Priestess?" O'Hara asked.

"In our religion, the celebrant is a female—it has a lot to do with what you might call the earth mother."

"Oh, yeah." O'Hara grinned. "Earth mother—should have thought of that myself."

"If you'll excuse me then?" Harold said, turning and leaving.

Frost looked at O'Hara. "Earth mother?"

"Yeah—what's an earth mother?"

"I'll tell you about it when you grow up," Frost told him.

"Shut up—both of you." Bess laughed. "Have some respect—listen—"

A chanting was starting, a chanting that was low but seemed to grow louder each time the chant was repeated; the persons in the circle around the fire swayed gently with it.

"Like a form of self-hypnosis," Bess murmured in Frost's left ear.

"Yeah—I can see that," he agreed. Watching men

48

and women in robes identical to those worn by the assassins at Julian Wells's house gave the one-eyed man the creeps. He kept expecting someone to pull a sword or a knife.

"I don't like this," O'Hara whispered too loudly.

Blanche Corrigan turned to O'Hara, saying, "Mike—it'll be all right. These people are like sincere religious people everywhere—gentle, kind, at this moment probably more interested in your understanding them than anything else. I was afraid, distrustful, the first time Dr. Wells took me to one of these."

As the chanting continued, Frost leaned across to her, asking, "Was Dr. Wells a witch—or whatever you call a male witch—what?"

"Some call them warlocks—but no. He was a very devout Catholic—went to weekday services during Lent, always closed the office on religious feasts. No, he wasn't a witch—just curious and tolerant."

Frost nodded, saying nothing.

The chanting stopped abruptly, the circle opening as a figure—he guessed a woman by the slender build—joined the circle, then passed through it into the center.

"The priestess," Frost murmured.

"I think so," Bess said.

"Who's that?"

Another figure was coming out of the circle; others in the circle turned, as if studying the figure themselves.

"Some kind of ritual?" Frost asked Blanche Corrigan.

"Nothing I've ever seen," she answered. "It looks like he's coming this way."

"What could—" Frost began, and as the figure moved, Frost pushed Bess down, going for his gun. "Look—"

The hooded figure held a pistol in the right hand, and there was a flash of gunfire, loud, the brilliance of the flash exaggerated because of the darkness around it.

As Frost hauled out the High Power, at the edge of his peripheral vision he could see Blanche Corrigan, her head snapping back, a tiny hole just above her left eye, her blond hair stained red with blood as the rear of her head seemed to explode outward.

Frost leveled the High Power, but the robed figure was too close to the circle of witches. Then he ran into the trees on the opposite side. Bess screamed.

O'Hara's big six-inch Metalifed Model 29 was raised in the air, the .44 Magnum booming once. "All right—none of you Satan-worshipin' creeps moves—FBI! First guy that twitches catches a .44 in the face!"

Frost looked at Bess, lying on the ground, her face whiter than he remembered it. "I'm going after the killer—stick with Mike." Frost started running, toward the coven of witches, shouting to O'Hara, "Mike—I think the rest of 'em are good guys—I'm goin' after the killer!"

"Frost—damn it—you guard the witches and I'll go after the killer!" O'Hara shouted.

"Can't hear ya," the one-eyed man called back, pushing his way through the knot of black-robed figures, past the ceremonial altar, past the bonfire, through the far arc of the circle of witches, then into the woods, after the killer. He figured that the killer had a sixty-second head start, and probably knew the woods, had rehearsed the ground. But it wasn't going to keep the one-eyed man from trying. . . .

The one-eyed man slowed, perhaps five hundred yards into the woods, hugging the slender trunk of one of the tall Georgia pines. He looked up—there really was moonlight coming through them.

Because of the heaviness of his own breathing—a five-hundred-yard dash across rough terrain, dodging tree trunks—he could hear nothing else for an instant. Then wind, perhaps. A tree branch snapped ahead of him, sounding loud in the stillness. Frost fired the High Power, twice, toward the sound of the breaking branch, then dodged right. The assassin had been right-handed, and would more naturally swing a gun left to acquire a target.

Frost waited.

There was no betraying, answering gunshot. "Smart," he murmured, starting forward, slowly. He wondered how smart. The one-eyed man reached up to a low-hanging branch, intentionally breaking it then dodging behind a different tree trunk and flattening himself against its slender shape as a gunshot echoed through the woods, a chunk of bark peeling off the tree trunk.

Frost had made the flash, but he knew better than to expect the gunman to wait for him to fire back.

Frost stepped from behind the tree trunk, the Metalifed High Power in both fists in a modified Weaver stance, his right first finger pumping the trigger in two-shot bursts, right, left, center, then right and left again.

Frost tucked back into the trees; answering gunfire hammered toward him. He had already dumped the magazine, changed sticks to a fresh one. One round still remained in the High Power's chamber, giving him fourteen before he had to change again.

The answering shots had been high, low, right and left; but only one shot in each direction, dirt kicking up, tree bark spraying. "Single-column pistol or no spare magazines," Frost conjectured to himself.

The gun had sounded like a 9mm, and the shots

51

that had been fired confirmed that.

Frost pumped two rounds, then ran forward, keeping low. Two more answering shots, then nothing.

He estimated that on the run he had gained fifteen yards, placing the gunman about twenty-five yards ahead.

"Football," he thought, remembering tackling Martin in the airport. "Martin?"

Something in his guts made him repeat the name. "Martin!"

Frost shouted it out. "Martin! I know it's you—can feel it—Martin!"

Two shots rang out, Frost closing his right eye against the fragments of tree bark that sprayed against his face.

"It *is* you!" the one-eyed man shouted, firing twice, then running. He gained another five yards before the gunman started firing again. Two more shots.

Frost had lost count, but if it was a double-column magazine pistol—another Browning, a Beretta or a Smith perhaps—then if there was no spare magazine, the killer would be nearly out.

Or—Frost started to run, firing two more shots, then throwing himself to the ground, a spray of rotted leaves and dirt kicking up around him as the gunman fired what sounded to Frost like at least ten shots.

"Well—so much for his running out of ammo," the one-eyed man muttered to himself, shrugging.

He pushed himself up, ran another five yards, and took cover behind some trees.

"Martin!"

Frost heard the sound of running, hard running, tree branches breaking, twigs snapping; and at the far edge of a wide shaft of moonlight, he thought he could make out a black shape, moving fast.

The one-eyed man pushed away from the trees and

started running himself, after the black-robed killer—Martin? It could have been a trap, to sucker him into a killing ground, but the one-eyed man kept running. Tree branches snapped at his face; the Browning, held ahead of him, warded off the larger ones. Frost ducked, dodging, catching another glimpse of the black-clad assassin.

The ground started breaking, dropping off. "A road," Frost rasped to himself.

Martin—if it was Martin—would have a car there. Frost leaned forward, hurling himself into the run, branches cracked from the force of his body, the force of the headlong lunge he now made.

The tree line ended and beyond it was a dark clearing. The moonlight cast bizarre shadows across its face.

Frost could see the man he pursued. The one-eyed man stopped, steadying himself, the Metalifed High Power locked in both fists, the thumb safety wiping off, his trigger finger pulsing—one shot, another, the High Power rocking in his hands.

The black-robed figure lurched forward, rolling down a low embankment.

Frost started forward, running again.

He mentally counted his shots—six left.

He reached the brow of the rise; beneath him there was an automobile—a Datsun 280ZX, fast, sleek, and black—black like the robe the killer wore.

"Martin?" Frost called out.

A burst of gunfire came from Frost's left—a searing pain in the left side of his neck as he rolled with it, toppling down the grade, crashing against a tree trunk, stunned.

He shook his head to clear it; the black-robed figure was up, running toward the automobile. Frost tried to raise his pistol but a stab of pain in the left side of his neck washed over him. He ran his left hand along the side of his neck. It came away sticky and wet with blood.

Frost pushed himself to his feet, then sagged against the tree trunk. The Datsun's lights came on; its engine roared to life.

The car was about twenty yards up the road from where Frost stood. The one-eyed man sucked in his breath hard. The Datsun started moving down the road. Frost raised the High Power, firing, firing—two shots, then three in a long burst. He pumped the trigger once more, the last 115-grain JHP homing toward the target. There was the sound of glass shattering, the slide of Frost's pistol locking open.

Not bothering to close it, Frost rammed the pistol into his belt, and ran toward the 280ZX. As he reached the road, the car came. Frost reached out for it, to grab onto something—one of the mirrors, the luggage rack. He reached for it but his hands barely touched the metal as it streaked past; Frost sagged into the road.

The one-eyed man lay there awhile, the pain in the side of his neck intense. Still, he was alive for the next round, he told himself.

Chapter Seven

Frost squirmed in the leather chair—leather or vinyl, he wasn't sure. The gunshot wound in the left side of his neck had been a bleeder and he'd nearly needed a transfusion. His head ached. He wasn't certain if it was the old head wound from Florida, the whack on the head from the night stick at the airport, or the pain in the side of his neck having moved up along a nerve ganglion. He shrugged, closing his eye against it.

"Are you with us, Mr. Frost?"

Frost opened his eye. "Yeah—I'm with you, Agent Cummins."

"Good—because this is important, for you, for Miss Stallman, and for Agent O'Hara as well."

Frost eyed Cummins, the neatly combed blond hair, the immaculately tailored suit. Frost decided the guy probably didn't carry his gun because it ruined the lines of his clothes.

"All right—Agent O'Hara."

"What?" Mike O'Hara muttered, looking down into his hands.

"There's the threat of a lawsuit by the Coven of Demetrius against the Justice Department and specific named individuals—myself as special agent in charge here and yourself, Agent O'Hara, as the man who pulled a gun and called those people, 'Satan-worshiping creeps' they say. Did you call them Satan-worshiping creeps?"

Frost answered for him. "No—he dropped the *g* sound at the end of worshiping—came out more like—"

"Shut up, will ya," O'Hara snapped, then turned to Agent Cummins. "Well—they *are* Satan worshipers."

"As a matter of fact they aren't," Cummins noted. "They considered that an insult. And then the matter of threatening to shoot the next one who moved—in the face?"

"Well—hell—you got three dozen weirdos in black robes and one of them pulls a gun and kills a woman right in front of your eyes—what would you have done?"

"When the police arrived, well—all of the Coven of Demetrius members were completely naked under their robes—as is their custom, I believe."

"Well—how was—"

"Supposed to know that? I don't know," Cummins said evenly. "There is a possibility that a written apology from yourself, explaining the circumstances, the trauma you endured when the woman was gunned down before your eyes—all of that—might persuade them not to follow through with the lawsuit."

"But—"

"The director called me on this—personally. Sent you his regards, said he understood the problems faced by field agents in situations such as this—but he specifically requested that you make an apology."

"Apologize, Mike," Bess whispered.

O'Hara looked at her. "I don't—"

"The lawsuit is for sixteen million dollars—violation of religious freedom, mental anguish, all sorts of things. Our lawyers have contacted their lawyers and a well-phrased apology might do the trick."

"All right," O'Hara snapped. "So—I'll apologize."

"Good," Cummins said, looking relieved, Frost

thought.

"Now," Frost asked him, "what about that guy being Martin?"

"I have no idea—and no way to tell. Empty cartridge cases picked up at the scene indicate there were two semiautomatic pistols fired, both 9 mms. A Browning High Power and a Smith & Wesson Model 59—from the firing-pin indentations. Slugs carved out of trees, and even the bullet from Miss Corrigan's head indicate the same. You use a High Power." Cummins picked up Frost's gun from the desk where it lay, an evidence tag hanging from its trigger guard. "And the assailant apparently used the Smith & Wesson. There were no fingerprints on the cartridge cases linked to the Model 59, so evidently the man who loaded it used gloves. No match with the firing-pin indentations, extractor markings; nothing yet. As for it being Martin, you admit yourself that this was only a guess. And, as you learned yesterday from the Atlanta police, there is at present no way of determining just who this Martin is and consequently no way of finding him."

"Stone wall," O'Hara observed.

"Stone wall," Cummins reiterated. "I'm not really a bad guy—honestly. I don't like O'Hara having to apologize, although honestly he should have used more caution in his language there at the scene. I appreciate the fact, Mr. Frost, that you risked your life to chase the killer, and you risked your life earlier in the same evening to save Dr. Wells from the fire. You've been under a great deal of strain, probably had more harrowing experiences in the last twenty-four hours than many men have in their entire lives. And Miss Stallman . . ." Cummins smiled at Bess; she smiled back, only faintly. "I know you have a story to do on Satan worshipers—and I've checked and the bu-

57

reau will help you as much as it can with information on mutilation murders linked to cult groups. But other than that, I'd say leave this thing alone. There is apparently a well-organized band of killers tied in with this thing. And if you—or you Mr. Frost,"—he looked at Frost again—"encounter them once more, it might well prove fatal. None of us would want that."

"That means get out of town on the next stage?" Frost asked, grinning.

Cummins laughed. "You're not a desperado, and I'm certainly not a town marshal—I'm just trying to offer useful advice to you both. I hope you take it. I'm a public servant—I can't make you take it."

"You want me out of town, too?" O'Hara asked.

"You had an assignment to interview Dr. Wells. The director wanted me to have you stay on that, perhaps check Wells's background. Use your own discretion. But he advised the same thing: don't get in over your head."

"I won't—I never do," O'Hara snapped, standing up.

"What about my gun?" Frost asked.

Cummins ripped the tag off the trigger guard. "It's yours—just take my advice so you don't need to use it."

They all shook hands with Cummins, Frost realizing Cummins was just passing on the advice of someone vastly higher up, whether he agreed with it or not. Frost had no intention of taking it.

Outside Cummins' office, O'Hara declared, "I can write that apology over a hamburger at lunch—"

"Just so it isn't under a hamburger." Bess smiled.

"Funny." O'Hara told her. Then, looking at Frost, "You guys wanna come over to the hospital with me—? I wanna check on Dr. Wells firsthand."

"You go, Frost. I'm supposed to meet with Dr.

Wells's assistant over at his office."

"I don't like you going alone," Frost told her.

"I'll be fine," she answered, touching his forehead gently, peering up at his face. "You need a rest. You look tired."

"I still don't—"

"I'll be fine," she repeated. "His offices are downtown, in a large office building. There'll be security there and everything. Relax. You go with O'Hara—at least that way I'll know you're out of harm's way."

"But—"

"I'm a big girl—now go on," she insisted.

Frost leaned down, kissing her, then said, "Just remember—be careful over there. With that guy Martin and all those fanatics on the loose . . ." He let the sentence hang—perhaps he thought, because he didn't understand what Martin could have to do with knife-wielding satanic cultists.

As they started walking toward the elevator bank, O'Hara said it. "One thing doesn't fit. A professional-quality guy like this Martin—or whoever it was last night that you chased through the woods, Frost. A professional-quality guy and these wackos runnin' around with swords and knives and carving on people. The two don't mesh."

"Horns of a dilemma," Bess observed.

"But I wonder if they're connected—or Martin is just using the satanic thing as a cover-up."

"God knows," O'Hara said then.

Frost looked at his friend, saying, "Or if God doesn't, maybe the other guy knows."

Chapter Eight

O'Hara had parked his car. Having turned down the visor that carried a card saying something about official business, he had left the car under the hospital main entrance portico. Frost accompanied him into the building. A police officer was on duty in the lobby and O'Hara walked over to him, flashed his badge, identified himself, and got directions to where Dr. Wells was being kept. It was intensive care.

They took the elevator up. Frost still wasn't fond of elevators.

A policeman sat on a folding chair near the elevator bank. O'Hara again showed his I.D., and the police officer gave directions. "Good and tight," O'Hara remarked as they walked past the nurses' station and into the intensive-care wing.

"The security? I've penetrated tighter."

"Good thing we're just dealin' with a bunch of bloodthirsty amateurs."

"And Martin," Frost advised. "You said it yourself—he's professional, whoever he is."

"Look Frost—this Martin stuff—people are gonna start thinkin'—"

"What? I'm fuzzy in the head? Uh-uh—it was him. And even if it wasn't, it was some kind of pro, some kind of guy who knew how to keep his cool; he tried suckering me. He was a veteran—of a lot of gunfights," Frost told him.

"Well, he isn't getting in here. You gave the Atlanta cops a description, right? And you sat down with the Identi-Kit operator at FBI headquarters this morning before our little talk with Cummins—so everybody's lookin' for Martin."

"But he probably doesn't look like that anymore," Frost said, his head starting to throb less. "If he knows I'm onto him, probably changed his appearance. Pros can do that—probably as good with make-up as an actor."

"He's still not gettin' in here—over there," and O'Hara gestured toward the end of the corridor, to where a policeman stood beside a door.

Frost gave up talking and walked the rest of the way with O'Hara in silence.

As they approached the door, it opened; the policeman turned around, looked at the nurse, then at O'Hara and Frost. The nurse—Oriental—smiled.

"Pretty girl," O'Hara said. "I like dark brown hair like that."

Then O'Hara pulled his I.D. one more time, showed it to the police guard at the door, and said, "Wanna see Dr. Wells. Can he talk?"

"The doctors say he's very weak, Agent O'Hara," the police officer—a black man in his mid-twenties—answered. "But I don't guess they'd mind y'all lookin' in on him."

"Thanks." Frost nodded, following O'Hara inside. There was a monitor unit above the bed, connected by tubes and wires to the shrunken figure swathed in bandages on the bed.

"He looks like—"

"Mike," Frost said, approaching the bed. He looked up at the monitor. "A wire's been pulled." Frost reached down, lifting up the loose lead from the machine. "These things are supposed to trigger the

61

people at the nursing station—but with the wire—"
Frost pulled back the sheet, covering Wells. The hospital gown was pulled down, and on the bare flesh over the heart there was a tiny puncture mark.

"Holy—" O'Hara gasped.

Frost looked at O'Hara, then said, "He's dead."

"Holy—"

"He's still dead—that nurse." Frost started for the door, O'Hara behind him. The one-eyed man scanned the far end of the hall through which they'd come; the pretty, brown-haired nurse was walking down it, carrying a covered tray in her hands.

"The dame!" O'Hara snapped.

"I'm gettin' her." Frost started to run, shouting back to O'Hara. "Seal off the building and get a doctor over here!"

The nurse turned around, puzzlement seemingly inscribed across her face. Then the tray dropped to the corridor floor; a pistol came from under the white towel draped over it.

Frost skidded on his heels toward a half-open doorway. The gun discharged, a chunk of the doorframe disintegrating beside his head.

Leaning out of the doorway, Frost pulled the Metalifed High Power. The nurse vanished around the corner. He started to run again, after her.

He reached the corner of the corridor and edged around it just in time to see a stairwell door closing. Frost raced toward it, the pistol in his right fist.

As he reached the door, O'Hara's voice came from the far end of the corridor, barking unintelligible orders. One of the nurses ran from the station, scarcely giving him or the gun in his hand a glance. A loudspeaker was dinging; then a woman's voice called, "Dr. Kelsoe—emergency. Dr. Kelsoe—"

Frost stepped back from the stairwell door, twisting

the knob, then throwing it open. There was no one on the landing. He dove in, almost skidding down the stairs, looking down, looking up, seeing no one. Then he heard it—the sound of heels clicking on the stairwell above him.

"The roof," he rasped, starting to run, taking the stairs three at a time, reaching the landing between floors, looking up, seeing a patch of white—the nurse's uniform—disappearing past the next landing.

Frost took the next flight of stairs, three at a time, running, not stopping on the next landing, keeping going. He made the next flight, stopping again between floors, starting to peer up the stairwell, then tucking back as he saw the flash of white clothing again. A shot zinged into the floor near his feet. Frost reached up, to return fire, but couldn't—the target was gone.

The one-eyed man started running again, up toward the next landing. He tried the door leading into the hall—it was locked, and he listened again.

The clicking of shoes against the stairs was gone—she could have just removed her shoes, he thought. He checked the doorway again, gambling, then started to run up the stairs, he hoped after her.

He made the next landing, between floors as usual; a skylight was visible now. And at the edge of the skylight he thought he saw a flash of white.

He took the next flight, again three steps at a time. He found a panic-locked door there.

Frost felt the tendons in his neck tighten; his palms sweat as he put his hand on the panic lock. The door gave slightly. Frost stepped back, kicking the panic bar; the door swung open wide. Frost waited; no shots came.

The door started slamming back, and Frost edged into the doorframe, catching the door, holding it open about a foot.

He peered out along the roof. Some small structures housed air-conditioning or heating equipment, and at the far end was a target painted in white and orange over black—a rooftop helipad.

Frost started through the doorway.

If the woman he sought was on the roof, she could be hiding behind the air-conditioning equipment. He left himself in the open, to draw her out, his guts churning as he started walking past the skylight.

The one-eyed man heard the crunch of gravel and wheeled, diving to the roof surface in the bright sunlight as he rolled. The nurse was standing beside one of the air-conditioning units, the pistol in her hands, firing. The cinders on the roof surface sprayed up. Frost fired two shots; the woman dived back behind the equipment.

Frost rolled again, coming up behind what looked like a metal storage shed. The door was locked. He leaned against the edge of the building, his head aching badly again, his right eye paining him.

Frost eased the muzzle of the High Power around the corner of the shed, firing twice; the nurse fired back—two more shots.

He wanted her alive more than dead—as a lead to Martin, as a lead into the fanatical Satanists.

"Give up," Frost shouted out; then lied. "Wells isn't dead. He's one of the statistically few people whose heart is on the right side. He was born that way."

Frost had no idea if that was really possible. "You hear me?"

Two more shots, then a clicking sound.

"Sucker," he called himself, running from the side of the building, toward the air-conditioning equipment beside which the nurse hid.

64

But he saw her running, the pistol held limply in her right hand.

She turned, trying to fire; Frost dodged right, rolling, but the gun in her hands was empty. Then—just as in the movies, he thought—she threw the pistol.

It hit the roof surface a yard from him; the one-eyed man eyed it as he got to his feet—a vintage European make which he couldn't instantly identify. He started after her, upping the safety on his pistol and ramming it into his belt.

The nurse was at the edge of the roof line now, nowhere to go.

Frost slowed, as she turned back to face him.

"Give it up, lady," he rasped.

She waited; Frost started toward her. He was within a yard of her when her hands moved, a massive lockblade folding knife coming out the pocket of her nurse's uniform, flashing open. The knife blade sliced the air inches from his face. Frost dropped, doing a leg sweep against her ankles; the woman crashed down, her skirt halfway up her thighs, the knife sliding across the roof surface.

But she was on her feet before Frost could jump her—and there was something decidedly different about her—her hair seemed to be falling off.

The nurse's left hand flashed up to the hair, ripping it away.

Heavily made up, but distinctly male—the nurse was a man.

"You—" Frost snarled. The man lunged for him now as Frost side-stepped, but the man's reflexes were too quick. A vicious sidearm blow hammered against Frost's rib cage.

Frost wheeled, turning half away; his right foot punched out for a double kick, into the chest.

As the "nurse" fell back, the false breasts he'd worn

65

became dislodged and created a bizarre lopsided effect under the dress.

But he was on his feet again, going into a flying kick, his right foot tucked under his body, his left snapping out. The foot hammered against Frost's left shoulder as he dodged; the concussion of the kick made the throbbing in his head worse.

Frost hit the roof's surface, rolling; the "nurse" started another flying kick.

Frost rolled; the man crashed down. Frost was on his feet, snapping a savate kick into the man's rear end, throwing him off balance.

Frost started for him, but the man was up, hands moving in some sort of cata, a low hiss coming from deep in his throat.

The man started to wheel, kicking. Frost side-stepped, past his guard, snapping out with his left foot, catching the man in the right side of the head. The man stumbled back; Frost started for him.

Then the man did something Frost hadn't counted on. He ran—straight toward the edge of the roof line—and dove—into space.

There was a scream, more like a laugh. Frost raced to the edge of the roof, peering over.

Beneath him, about five stories down, there was the beginning of a concrete wall, perhaps an addition to the hospital. The rust-covered metal skeleton for the concrete extended up about ten feet. Impaled on at least a half-dozen of these, his white nurse's uniform splotched red with blood, was the killer, face up, eyes staring.

Frost, hearing movement on the roof behind him, turned and saw Mike O'Hara.

"What happened?" O'Hara asked. Three police officers, one of them the black man who had been posted at Wells's room, ran up after him.

Frost didn't answer for a moment; his head throbbed. "Bess was right—I need rest—but I can't."

"What?"

"Just did the Dutch act."

"Suicide?" O'Hara said incredulously.

"Here . . ." Frost reached down, picked up the dark brown wig from the roof surface, and handed it to O'Hara. "You liked her hair so much—have it."

Frost lit a cigarette, his hands trembling.

Chapter Nine

O'Hara came back from the telephone. "I couldn't reach Wells's office—line was busy. So I called security in the building there—told me Bess had gone up and nothin' funny was goin' on."

"I just got a feeling," Frost said, stubbing a cigarette into the ashtray beside the elevator bank. "Can I borrow your car?"

"That's an F.O.U.O.*—I can't."

"Do it anyway," Frost asked.

"Here—you're stealin' my keys, in case you get in trouble."

"Ride herd on the cops—I'll talk to 'em later." Frost nodded, taking the keys and starting to punch an elevator button, but the elevator doors opened.

"Relax—she's O.K." O'Hara called after him.

"Feeling again," Frost called back, the closing doors cutting off O'Hara's response.

He wasn't quite sure what it was—maybe just the headache, the pain in the left side of his neck, or having seen the phony nurse kill himself deliberately. He hated being up against fanatics. It reminded him of Vietnam, of stories his father had told him about Korea—people who ran onto a bayonet to blunt it so the guys behind them could kill you. The thought made him shake, or perhaps it was just fatigue. The

*F.O.U.O.—For Official Use Only

elevator doors opened and he stepped out into the hospital lobby. As he walked past one of the cops there, the policeman gave him a nod—one of the men from the roof who'd come up with O'Hara.

Frost went outside. O'Hara's car was still parked under the portico. Frost dodged a taxicab, walked across to the car, opened the door, and stood beside it for a moment before entering. He could try calling Bess at Wells's office. Probably nothing—just a busy phone line. His head ached and he was tired.

He slid in behind the wheel—the feeling that something was wrong, the vibes, even stronger now.

He turned the key—the gas tank was more than half full by the way the needle rose.

He released the emergency brake, threw the transmission into drive.

He sat under the portico, his foot on the brake, the engine rumbling. Under other circumstances, he would have called this feeling a sixth sense, the thing that caused the tiny hairs on the back of his neck to rise, warning of danger or someone watching. He had learned over the years—sometimes the hard way—not to ignore this feeling, whatever caused it.

He had seen the feeling work in reverse, with sentries he had removed; suddenly, for no reason, they could feel you were coming for them. The one-eyed man lit a cigarette, unable to decide—his head aching.

The window of O'Hara's car had already been rolled down; Frost saw no sense in O'Hara's having locked the door. Force of habit, he decided. Habit—his own habit was to heed his instincts, no matter how stupid it seemed.

The one-eyed man snapped the butt of the Camel out the open window, into the driveway, glanced to his right and hit the switch for O'Hara's Mars light and siren. Starting from the portico, heavy-footed on the gas, he screeched to a halt at the end of the driveway, then cut a sharp left across the flow of traffic, accelerating, the car weaving, underpowered for what he was trying to do.

But his headache stopped as he stomped the gas pedal to the floor; the wheel straightened as he started down the street.

The office building was at the far side of town, just inside the perimeter so Frost took a one-way street left—going the wrong way—toward the expressway. Then he made a right, running a stop sign and crossing heavy traffic into the expressway feeder ramp. The siren still wailed, the Mars light flashed.

He accelerated down the ramp, stomping the brakes, skidding, sliding onto the shoulder as traffic from behind him on the expressway zigged and zagged around him. "No damned acceleration ramps—poor excuse for a—" He didn't bother finishing the epithet about the expressway system, but instead edged the car forward along the shoulder. Honking the horn, flicking the siren on and off, he leaned out the window, reaching his left hand out to signal his entry into the lane; when it was clear, he wrenched the wheel into a hard left, then a hard right recovery. He stomped the gas pedal, weaving through the lanes of midday traffic; the speedometer hovered between sixty and seventy as he drove. It would take ten minutes or less to reach the perimeter if the traffic didn't block up. Frost stomped the gas pedal harder, his headache gone now but the sixth-sense feeling stronger than before. . . .

The one-eyed man simultaneously crunched the brake pedal and cranked the selector into park. The car lurched, skidding slightly beside the curb as he killed the ignition switch, the siren, and then started out the door. He slid out on the passenger side beside

70

the curb. Running toward the office-building entrance, he looked up toward the top floor where Wells had his offices and saw nothing peculiar.

He reached the center revolving doors—they were locked. Cursing, he tried the side door. It was locked as well.

An old security guard—white-haired, overweight, and florid-faced—looked up, then started to stand up and meander toward the doors.

Frost pulled a credit card from his wallet. Working it into the door latch he pulled the door open with his fingernails and raced past the security guard.

"Hey—you!"

"Mr. Wells's offices—trouble up there—hurry!"

Frost reached the elevator banks, punched the buttons, and waited, hammering his fist against the wall. The old security guard was still coming. "Who the heck are you, mister?"

"I'm working with the FBI," Frost said half-truthfully—he was working with one FBI agent.

"Well—why the heck didn't ya say so?" The guard smiled. The elevator door opened; Frost stepped inside, pushing the floor button, pushing the button to close the doors. The old man shouted, "Hey—wait for me!"

Frost held the door open a second with his hands, the door ricocheting off his fist then starting to close again as the security guard stepped inside. Frost pushed the floor button again.

"Will this express up to the top floor?"

"Nobody else but them in the building—hey—what the heck's goin' on, anyways?"

"Never mind, sir," Frost told him. "Just keep your gun handy there."

There was a light in the old man's eyes; his right hand, trembling slightly, touched the yellowed ivory

71

butt of a worn blue revolver carried in a seen-better-days holster on his right hip.

"What is it?" the old man asked. "Commies?"

"Satanists," Frost told him.

"Ya mean—ya mean folks that prays to the devil?"

"I don't know if they pray to him—but I guess they work for him."

The elevator doors opened, and Frost stepped out. At the far end of the hallway he saw glass doors; printing on the doors read: WELLS INVESTMENT ASSOCIATES.

"Wells was—"

"Writer and a stockbroker," the old security guard offered.

Frost started toward the doors, a sinking feeling in the pit of his stomach. He had been wrong; O'Hara would holler about misuse of the car; probably O'Hara would get into trouble—Bess would be—

He stopped, peering through the doors to the carpeted floor of the outer office.

"I don't see nothin' wrong," the old security guard volunteered.

"I do!" Frost started for the doors—the ring he had given Bess was on the office floor.

He tried the doors—they were locked.

"Stand back, friend," Frost told him, then started away from the doors.

As Frost spun, the old security guard gave him a strange look. Frost's left foot snapped out against the glass doors where they joined; the doors shattered. The one-eyed man recovered, back-stepping as glass sprayed into the office.

Frost snapped the Browning High Power from its Cobra shoulder rig and started through the doorway, stepping across the largest piece of glass, reaching down to pick up the ring.

72

"Look out!"

It was the old security guard. Frost wheeled. Behind him, a man ran toward him, black-robed, wielding a sword. Frost side-stepped; the sword crashed down against a typewriter. The carriage, lopped off, slid to the floor.

Frost raised his pistol to fire, but there was a booming sound to his left.

The old security guard had his revolver out, firing once, then once again. The robed figure with the sword crumpled forward across the desk.

"Thank you!" Frost called out, starting toward the rear of the office, Bess's ring safely stored in his pants pocket, the High Power in his right fist.

He smelled something, then turned to the side office to his left, kicking open the door. "Smoke."

Then he heard a scream. "Frost!"

Frost turned right, racing down the small hallway toward the rear office—Wells' office?

He started to kick in the door, but stepped back. The center of the door split, a heavy sword blade having cut through it.

Frost couldn't fire so he let the section of door against the latch fall outward. First one, then two more sword-wielding robed figures started through, toward him.

Frost side-stepped, so he'd have a backstop. He pumped the trigger of the High Power twice, gut-shooting the nearest man, the body lurching forward. Frost dodged the sword. Another sword gouged into the wall beside his head.

Frost tried getting his pistol free of the body, but couldn't. The two men came for him.

He let loose of the pistol and picked up the dead man's sword, slicing it high and right, blocking the downsweep of the sword from the nearest of the two robed killers.

Frost backed up, heard the boom of the security guard's gun again. Frost glanced behind him. One man stumbled through the hallway and fell; a second, wielding a sword, charged toward the old security guard.

Frost dodged left; one of the two sword-wielding killers was coming for him again. He deflected the lunge, back-stepping again.

"What the hell am I doing with a sword?" he asked himself.

The security guard's gun fired again. Frost, parrying a sword cut, glanced over his shoulder. The old man had hit the man with the sword who had been coming at him, but the man had kept coming as he died.

Frost shuddered for an instant. The old man's head had been half-cut from the trunk of his body; his neck was pumping gouts of blood as his body sagged to the floor, dead.

"You son of a—" Frost started back toward the old man, fighting off the two robed killers who were still coming for him.

He reached down into the blood, prying the man's dead fingers free of the old service revolver—a Colt Official Police with what looked like a five-inch barrel.

Frost fired the revolver once, point-blank, the .38 Special round slamming into the head of the nearest of the two swordsmen. His body rocked back and down, the robed killer behind him back-stepping. Frost thought perhaps he was temporarily shocked.

"One on one, now, asshole!" Frost snapped, raising the sword in his hands.

The swordsman began what looked like a martial-art cata with the sword. The heavy blade twirled through the air, slicing, feigning. Frost eyed the sword

74

in his own hands. Like the one his opponent carried, it was single-edged, with a blade perhaps a yard long, slightly curved, and with a Bowie-like false edge near the tip. The guard just in front of Frost's hands was heavy, ornate. Frost back-stepped as the swordsman came for him. The sword still danced in the man's hands; he feigned cuts and parries.

Frost felt himself grin, as he held the sword almost bolt upright about eighteen inches from his body.

The swordsman lunged, his blade sweeping left to right across Frost's body plane.

Frost parried it with his own blade, rolling the steel away, side-stepping, hacking with the sword blade, but only hacking air as the swordsman side-stepped and lunged again.

Frost brought his own sword down, blocking the thrust for his groin, pushing his opponent's blade off his own.

The smell of smoke from the small office was stronger now and soon, Frost realized, he'd be fighting flames as well as swords.

Bess screamed again. "Frost!"

The one-eyed man edged back; the swordsman came for him. Frost hacked outward with the sword, then dropped it. Snatching up the remainder of the electric typewriter that had been hacked to pieces earlier, he threw the typewriter console toward the swordsman. The machine thudded against the man's chest, knocking him back. Frost dived for him, his left knee crushing the swordsman's wrist under his body weight, keeping the sword and the right hand that held it motionless. Frost's fingers knotted around the man's neck.

Frost's thumbs pressured the windpipe; the swordsman's eyes bulged, his free left hand flailing upward toward Frost's face. Frost increased the pressure; the

75

man's mouth opened, his tongue started to roll out, and the skin of his face purpled to almost the color of a grape. Frost kept squeezing, a rattling sound, a gurgling sound, the eyes bulging still more, the tongue fully out now.

Frost loosened the pressure; the man gasped for breath. He punched the man once hard across the jaw, then again. The man's head lolled to the side. Frost pushed himself to his feet, stumbling back; he wasn't a murderer yet.

He reached down, grabbed up the sword he'd dropped, and started back down the hall. The small office was a mass of flames now. Frost went past it, en route fishing his Metalifed High Power from under the body of the dead swordsman in the hallway.

The High Power in his left hand, Frost took the sword and quickly looked above him at the ceiling. He'd seen it done in countless movies, always secretly wanted to try it. He took the sword and thrust it upward, letting it go, launching it toward the ceiling, to stick there and vibrate just like—

He dodged back; the sword bounced off the ceiling tile and plummeted back toward him, almost impaling his left foot.

"Gee!"

Just shaking his head, switching the pistol to his right fist, the one-eyed man started toward the office at the end of the corridor. Another illusion shattered, he thought sadly.

He reached the small office. Through its chopped-open door he could see Bess, hands tied to the arms of a chair, ankles bound, the chair tipped over on its side.

Slumped in the corner of the room was another woman, her hands and feet bound.

Frost started for Bess. "Frost—they've got fire

bombs planted."

"The one in that side room fizzled—no explosion, just a fire," Frost told her, taking the little Gerber knife and cutting her wrists free, then bending to her ankles and cutting the ropes there.

"You've got a run in your stockings," he told her.

"I'll buy a new pair." She smiled. "Mary!"

Frost followed her glance toward the woman slumped in the corner. "Mary—right." Frost moved over toward the woman, cutting her wrists free then rolling her over.

Dark-haired, pretty, the woman's eyelids fluttered. "Work on waking her up!" Frost commanded Bess, as he bent to cut the ropes on the woman's ankles. "She doesn't have a run."

"Bite it." Bess laughed.

"Such terrible language," Frost told her, then he helped Bess get the woman up into a sitting position. "What happened?"

"They just burst in here—she had a gun in the desk and started to—"

"Get the gun," Frost told Bess, "and get your purse, her purse—whatever. We gotta get the hell out of here."

Bess said nothing, but went straight to the desk. Frost watched her as she searched the drawers, finally opening the center one. "Here," she said, holding up something that at a distance Frost determined to be a Smith & Wesson Model 36 Chiefs' Special. "How do you open this thing?"

"Colts open by pulling the cylinder release catch back, and Smiths open by pushing forward."

"Which brand is this—must be Smith & Wesson," she said, opening the revolver, then slamming it closed. "Loaded."

"See if she had any spare ammo in the desk," Frost

77

advised, gently slapping the cheeks of the unconscious woman with the tips of his fingers. "Wake up, miss—wake up." Then he looked at Bess, asking, "What'd you say her name was?"

"Mary—Mary Boles."

Frost looked at the woman, again slapping her gently, trying to rouse her. "Mary—come on! Snap out of it—gotta wake up! Mary—Mary Boles!" The woman's eyelids fluttered, then opened. She looked up into his face, terror in her eyes. "Relax—I'm a friend—friend of Bess's."

"Bess?" She shook her head.

"Mary—" Bess dropped to her knees beside the woman. "This is Hank Frost—my fiancè—the man I told you about. He saved us."

Mary Boles's eyes closed, then opened wide. "I—I think—my God—my head—"

"They hit you," Bess told her. "I was afraid they'd killed you."

"We've gotta get out of here—can you walk?" Frost asked the woman.

"I—think—I think I can."

"Just keep saying that." Frost started helping her to her feet.

Tongues of flame licked periodically from the small side office into the corridor as Frost, supporting Mary Boles slumped against him, started toward the office door with Bess beside him. "Frost," Bess almost screamed, "the fire!"

"Gotta go through," Frost told her.

He looked behind him, around the office. Then he looked at Mary Boles. "Did Mr. Wells have a private bathroom here?"

The woman, still seeming groggy, nodded her head, not answering verbally but pointing to a small door at the far side of the office. "Bess—hold her up," Frost snapped, letting the woman slump against Bess as he ran across the office toward the bathroom. He ripped the door open, found the light switch, and started to search for towels. Bath towels—he found them in a cabinet beside the toilet. He pulled them out, then turned on the shower head, soaking them. He ran back across the office, leaving the water running and the lights on in the bathroom. "Here," Frost rasped, taking one of the sodden towels and draping it across Bess's head.

"My hair—"

"Cover your face and arms as much as possible, breathe through the towel. Help her." Frost commanded.

He draped the third towel over his own head, taking the weight of Mary Boles against him, then rasping, "The hell with it!" He hauled the woman up into his arms. "Let's go," Frost snapped, then started forward, down the corridor, tongues of flame now whipped across it in regular, almost clocklike patterns. "Follow me, kid," he shouted to Bess.

He waited, a tongue of flame licking outward, scorching at his hands where he carried the woman in his arms; then he darted forward, past the flames, Bess behind him.

They were past the office now and Frost shrugged the towel down from his head to around his shoulders. "Try the stairwell outside," Frost shouted, running as best he could with the woman in his arms. "Don't wait for me—get to the stairs—should be fireproof."

"I'm waiting for you," Bess cried out, staying beside him and slightly ahead as they reached the end of the corridor. He saw her look down at the partially decapitated security guard. "My God," she murmured, sucking in her breath.

"I got the guy up here. He saved my life. Damn

these people!" Frost cursed.

They started across the outer office toward the shattered glass doors. There was smoke in the hallway, but apparently blowing out from the office behind them.

"Fire alarm on the wall there—hit it," Frost shouted to Bess. She took the tiny hammer, broke the glass, then pulled the switch. The alarm was sounding now in the building corridor near the elevator banks. Frost couldn't be certain whether their alarm or the smoke had triggered it. Almost simultaneously, from the corridor ceiling, water sprayed down.

"Thank God for small favors," Frost shouted, staring toward the stairwell door.

"I'll get it," Bess shouted.

"Wait!" Setting Mary Boles down, Frost pushed her aside with his shoulder. The woman coughed, choking in his arms. "Take care of her."

Frost approached the door, touching its surface gingerly with the tips of his fingers. It wasn't warm. "Could be a fireproof door, but there could be fire on the other side—take her back a few feet," Frost commanded.

There was a panic lock on the door and Frost kicked at it. The lock depressed, and the door swung outward into the stairwell landing. There was no flame, no smoke.

Frost turned around, grabbing up Mary Boles into his arms, ordering Bess, "Come on, kid—down the stairs—hug the wall side, but watch out for heat—hurry!"

Bess started down ahead of him, Frost following with the woman in his arms. "Help me," he told Bess at the first landing. Setting Mary Boles down, he propped her on her feet; Bess held her up. Frost shouldered into her, getting the woman up across his left shoulder, holding her in position with his left hand, balancing the weight with his right arm as he started down the stairs again, this time ahead of Bess.

The sprinklers in the stairwell suddenly started to work, their fine spray drenching them and making the surface of the stair treads slippery underfoot as the one-eyed man continued downward, Bess immediately behind him. "Watch your footing," he told her.

He gauged that they were paralleling the farthest elevator shaft as they descended. The heat from the wall was getting progressively greater as they continued. "That shaft—must be on fire," he shouted as they reached another landing.

"Thank goodness we didn't take the elevator," Bess called back.

"Could still burn through—maybe," Frost nodded, catching his breath, then continued downward.

Smoke was filling the shaft of the stairwell as they descended. From behind him, Bess pulled up the wet towel over Frost's head again. The one-eyed man's right eye teared, his breathing was hard, he began coughing, his body suddenly racked with it.

He stopped, bending over, a few stairs above the next lower landing. "Frost? Are you—"

"I'm—" Frost started. The stairs under him shuddered; a booming sound assailed his ears, making them ring in the confined space. He started to fall forward, throwing his weight back. Bess tugged at him as the landing below them belched up flame, huge chunks of it bursting upward.

The one-eyed man fell backward, sprawling on the steps. "See if she's O.K.," Frost ordered Bess. Chunks of debris now plummeting down, Frost shielded both women as best he could with his body. He felt pain between his shoulder blades, on his left thigh; the scorching heat of the flames made it hard for him to breathe. As he looked up, he felt a chunk of

81

debris fall from his back.

Below him, when he looked downward, the landing was gone, and a ragged hole in the wall belched fire from the elevator shaft. "Must have fire-bombed an elevator," Frost snapped.

"How could those people have—" Bess started.

"Probably came in wearing business suits, carried the robes and swords in some way—may have been in the office since last night—I don't know. But something Dr. Wells had they wanted, or they at least didn't want anyone else to get it."

"Do you think," Bess shouted, coming into his arms, the head of the injured woman on her lap, "that the terrorist group he wanted to tell the FBI about could have been these people—Satanists?"

"Maybe—I'll tell ya one thing—I don't just think they're a bunch of wackos anymore," Frost told her, standing up. The staircase sagged under him as he shifted his weight. "Shit—we can't stay here, and if we start up—"

"Can we climb down?" Bess asked her.

"Don't know—try," he rasped. He reached to his trouser belt, undoing the buckle, pulling the belt free of the loops. "Gimme that towel, and the one she's got," Frost ordered.

He snatched the towel that covered his own head, twisting the wet cloth into a rope, then knotted it with the towel Bess had worn to protect her own face. His eye streamed tears from the smoke and he coughed; the smoke was denser now and he felt it more because of the lack of the wet towel that had filtered the air he'd breathed. Bess handed him the third towel, and he knotted it to the other two. "Here—slip this belt around you, so it comes up under your armpits. I'll tie the end of the towels to it and lower you down."

"I can—"

"Don't argue. You slip the harness off, I'll pull it back up, then lower Mary Boles to you."

"What about you, Frost?" she pleaded, tears streaming from her green eyes.

"I'll let myself down—hitch the belt to one of the railing supports. Don't worry—just hurry up with the belt," Frost told her.

He helped her secure the belt in place, then knotted the end of one of the towels to it. "Now—you'll have to get over the railing." She tried raising her leg to climb over it. The skirt she wore wouldn't allow it. Frost reached down to the hem, found the seam along the side of the skirt and ripped. "There—now." Frost helped her clamber over the railing which shuddered under her comparatively meager weight.

Frost held her there with his right hand, shifting the rope of towels down to the base of the railing, where it met the stairs. "Now—let yourself go—protect your head with your hands in case you spin against the stairwell," he shouted.

She looked into his face a moment, then leaned across the rail, kissing him quickly on the mouth. "If anything—"

"It won't." He smiled, then started lowering her, her body spinning as the towels started to untwist.

"Frost!"

"It's all right—just protect your face," he shouted to her, lowering her into the smoke, hearing the choking sounds from her. "Tell me when you're down."

"Not—not yet," she called up.

"Tell me—"

"Not—wait—I feel it. I'm—" The rope of towels was at its maximum extension. He let out a long hard sigh. "I'm down."

"Quick—get the harness off. I'll lower Mary Boles down," he called back.

He pulled up the weightless harness, getting it through the railing spars. He turned to Mary Boles. Her breathing was labored, irregular. He inhaled, leaning over her, cocking her head back, giving her his own breath several times until her chest began to rise and fall more regularly. He cinched the belt around her, under her armpits, then dragged her across the stairs, toward the railing.

The staircase trembled under him as he again shifted his weight in order to get the unconscious woman over the railing. He held her with difficulty, as he fed the rope of towels through the railing at its base; then he released her slowly, starting to lower her into the smoke. He called out, "Bess—check her breathing when she gets through that crap!"

"All right," Bess called up.

Then Mary Boles was lost inside the cloud of smoke. Frost reached the end of the rope of towels, feeling a tugging at it, the rope almost coming away from his hands. Then there was no weight. "I've got her," Bess called up.

"I'm coming down," Frost shouted, coughing as he did. The smoke was more intense now, and flames belched from the hole near the elevator shaft. Doused by the sprinkler system, his hair plastered across his forehead, he leaned his head back, trying to breathe.

He pulled up the rope of towels, then began to secure his trouser belt around the railing. He tugged at the belt, pulling against the supports of the railing. The railing gave way.

"Look . . . out . . . the railing!"

There was a scream from below him. Frost leaned over the shuddering staircase, trying to peer into the smoke. "Bess!"

"I'm all right—it just missed us. What will you do?"

"Don't know yet," he shouted. "Anyway—I didn't lose my belt!"

Frost separated the belt from the rope of towels and threaded it back around his waist as he searched the stairwell, looking for something to which he could attach the rope of towels. On the landing above him he saw it— "Stupid," he shouted.

"What?" Bess called.

"Stupid—I'm stupid," he shouted back, starting up the staircase. The stairs shuddered under him, swaying. He stood, stock-still, motionless. Less than a dozen feet away on the landing above, was a fire hose inside a glass case. He could have used it to let Bess and Mary Boles down to safety. He started coughing, took one of the towels, unknotted it, and put the still damp towel over his head and across his face.

He stuffed the other towels into the pockets of his ruined suit; then he tried moving up the stairs again. The stairway heaved under him, a cracking, tearing sound, metal striking against metal assailing his ears.

He dropped, flattening himself against the staircase; the shuddering of the stairs under him stopped.

He started to crawl, slowly, along the stairs, toward the landing above and the fire hose there on the wall.

The heat was now his worst enemy, his breathing more difficult than before.

"Bess . . . get out . . . go down the stairs. . . . Don't wait—"

"Not without you," she cried.

"Do what I say, damn it!"

"When did I ever? No!" she shrieked.

"Bess—I might not—"

"Then neither of us will," she called.

Frost coughed, inching up the stairs. "You got—" He coughed again. "Got Mary Boles to think of—not just us!"

85

"No!"

"Women," he murmured. His extended left hand touched the landing surface at the head of the stairs. He pulled himself up, slowly, not daring to stand on the landing, instead crawling across its surface instead, toward the fire-hose case on the wall.

Inside the case as he looked up he could see an ax and what appeared to be thirty, perhaps fifty feet of fire hose. He got to his knees under it, then to his feet, hugging the wall. "The glass," he murmured. The one-eyed man reached under his sodden suitcoat, snatching the Metalifed High Power from the Cobra rig there.

He turned the pistol around in his hands, holding it in his left fist by the slide. Turning his face away, with the butt of the pistol he hammered the glass, hearing it shatter. He looked back, using the pistol butt again to hammer away the broken glass from the edges of the case.

The hose. He started to uncoil it as he rammed the Metalifed High Power into his waistband. It wasn't connected to anything, but it was at least thirty feet long. Flat—gray in color. He coiled the hose on his left shoulder, then dropped to his knees, then to his belly, crawling across the landing, smoke surrounding him now, cutting visibility to where he could barely see a yard ahead of him. By feel, his lungs aching, his head reeling, he found the edge of the landing, reached up, and found the railing. He started to touch it, then murmured, "Please, God!" He reached for the railing supports and tugged, pulled, pushed—the railing held.

"Thank you," he murmured, taking the hose from his left shoulder, coughing as he wound the nozzle end around the railing supports, intertwining it, figuring if one support gave way one of the others would hold his weight.

He knotted the hose with a square knot, then another massive square knot over it.

"I'm—I'm letting down a hose—can you—"

"Yes," Bess shouted, coughing. "I can see it."

"Hold the end of it—I'm starting down," he called out.

He pushed himself to his feet beside the railing, the landing creaking under him. "If the landing goes—or the section of staircase—run for it. Leave Mary Boles if you have to—better than both of you—"

"Hurry," Bess screamed. "There's fire down here —the wall behind me is buckling with it—might burst through any second."

"Get out!"

"No—damn it—no!" she screamed.

"Remind me to—" He didn't finish the sentence, coughing, and wondering, too—slap her or kiss her?

Gingerly, he straddled the railing, then pulled his left foot behind him, over it, holding the length of fire hose—his life line. He crouched by the edge of the railing, let his right foot down, then his left, his legs swinging free as, hand over hand, he started to lower himself into the smoke. His eye teared, his lungs seemed to burn, and nausea swept over him; his head ached. "Come on," he rasped, talking to himself. "One hand over the other—come on." He kept moving, his knees hugging at the fire hose, his feet entwined in it, his hands slowly, methodically lowering him downward.

This took an interminable time, but finally he felt something touch at his ankles, and in the almost ghostly haze of smoke he shuddered. Then he felt it again—hands on his legs, on his rear end, on his back. "Come on, Frost—come on," Bess almost cooed to him. He could feel a railing under him, against him, arms folding around him as he half-fell across her body, choking.

"Air," he rasped. He sank to his knees, felt her cocking his head back, sensed her mouth on his, smothering him. He was choking as she breathed into his lungs.

The one-eyed man coughed, lurching forward. On the stairs beside him was another figure—Mary Boles.

Frost handed Bess one of the two wet towels, still stuffed in his pockets.

"Help—help me get her—"

Frost pushed himself to his knees, then to his feet, reaching down into the smoke for Mary Boles. Bess pulled the unconscious woman up; Frost shouldered her. He lurched under the weight, sagging forward, his knees buckling, but Bess was beside him, her arms around him, her hands helping him as he started down the stairs.

They moved, slowly, tortuously; and after a time —he didn't know how long—there was an explosion from above. Flaming chunks of debris rained down on them. Bess, looking ridiculous with the wet towel over her head, held him tight.

He stopped looking at the floor markings on the stairwell landings they passed, telling himself instead that each step he took meant one less to take. He glanced at his watch as his left hand locked again on the knees of the unconscious woman across his left shoulder. How long had it been? His head ached.

"One foot—left, right," he muttered.

"Frost?"

"Left—right—left," he moaned, moving his feet.

He felt a coolness, the sudden change in temperature making him nauseous. He threw up onto the stairs, heaving forward with it, then holding himself against the railing. "I'll carry her," Bess said.

88

"No—left—right," he continued, almost like a chant.

The coolness was increasing, the air almost fit to breathe now— "Frost—we're down," Bess told him.

"Left—right," he continued, lurching toward the doorway that Bess was feeling with her hands.

"It's not hot!"

She opened the door. Frost, beside her, squeezed through it with her.

There was light amid the sound of fire engines, men rushed toward them.

Frost stopped and stood, breathing. As soon as two firemen grabbed the woman from his shoulder, he fell forward, blackness washing over him.

Chapter Ten

"You know,"—Frost smiled, holding Bess's arm partially for support, mostly out of affection—"I've been hospitalized for tons of things—mostly various gunshot and knife wounds—never smoke inhalation, though." He laughed, coughing slightly.

"Thank God you're all right now," Bess told him as she opened the car door. He slid into the front passenger seat. Then he fired a wave at the nurse by the hospital door, a wheelchair still in front of her. She smiled and blew him a kiss.

As Bess slipped behind the wheel, she said, "What was that about?"

"She liked bathing me," Frost told her. "That's all. I guess she liked my skin or something."

"Hmm—or something," Bess answered, turning the key in the ignition. The rented Ford's engine rumbled to life. "Are you sure you're up to it?"

"What—going to Mary Boles's house for dinner?"

"Uh-huh."

"You just fill my glass for me when I need it and I'll be fine." He started to light a cigarette; Bess held the hand with the light for a second.

"Should you—?"

"This is the kind of smoke inhalation I like—I'll be fine," he assured her, lighting the first cigarette he'd had in forty-eight hours or more—choking with the first puff, feeling slightly light-headed, but then inhaling again. It was better the second time. He said, coughing, "Anyway—gotta see if Mary Boles knows anything about those—"

"The police were guarding you because of them," Bess told him. "I don't know—this was my assignment Frost—you don't—"

"Sure. Just let you loose alone for those creeps to get at? Not on your life, kid," he answered, inhaling again. "Besides—they tried killing me too—and there's that old security guard. I gotta pay those suckers back for him, too. No—I'll be fine. O'Hara's gonna be there?"

"Yes," Bess answered softly. "O'Hara's going to be there. He hasn't gotten any fresh leads. What they were able to recognize from the bodies of the dead men in the office building—none of them appeared to have any connection to each other; none of them were known to be satanic cultists; none of them even had criminal records."

Frost suddenly noticed the ring on her finger. "Hey —remember all the trouble we went through with that?" he asked.

"Uh-huh—I do."

"Well—a few crazies don't change things—we'll get 'em together." He smiled.

She looked across at him, then took her right hand from the wheel to put it on his left thigh. He covered her right hand with his left.

"I've been doing some research—hard to do, really," Bess began. "There's a ton of information about witches—not much on true Satanists. The FBI stuff—at the National Criminal Justice Reference Center—doesn't even keep statistics on mutilation murders as a separate research subject; and the FBI doesn't even have mutilation deaths in their Washington computers."

91

"Sort of virgin ground, huh," Frost commented.

"More than you might think—virgins. Satanists use unbaptized children and virgins as their victims—sometimes they eat them according to some of the literature."

Frost just looked at her. "Makes me glad you're not a virgin." Frost laughed.

Bess simply shuddered. "If these people are for real—then—God, I don't know what we're up against," she said softly.

"I don't think they run around eating people in the twentieth century. Probably do all sorts of weird dances, light fires, dance around naked—that kinda crap—then go kill people for kicks. Maybe high on drugs."

"Frost,"—she shuddered again, her hand squeezing his left thigh more tightly—"it's just—just that I—I don't think we're up against ordinary people. These aren't—"

Frost turned in his seat, studying her face. "Look, kid—when you cut them, they bleed; when you shoot them, they fall down—that's good enough for me."

"But—"

"Fanatics—they're crazy, high—whatever, but they're still human. There's no such thing as the supernatural—at least not with any of these clowns. I kill them, they stay killed. And I figure before we're through if I'm lucky I'll get the chance to kill a lot more of them."

"Frost—I'm afraid. I've been afraid before; I'll be afraid again—but never like this. Mary Boles—she had two guns—gave me that one she had in her desk."

"That's illegal. Don't tell O'Hara. He'd probably bust you. You're not a Georgia resident."

"I don't care. I'm keeping it in my purse until this thing is over."

Frost stubbed out his cigarette in the ashtray at the middle of the dashboard, then leaned across and kissed her cheek. "I just hope you don't have to take that gun out of your purse," he told her. . . .

Bess parked the car almost at the base of the stone house's front steps, then insisted that Frost wait for her while she came around to help him out. He resented being treated that way, but realized he was still weak and actually did have trouble walking. It was the smoke inhalation, coupled with the headaches he'd been having—and a low-grade infection. These had severely debilitated him. It had been tough enough telling the doctors to let him out of the hospital. Frost had promised virtually everything to get them to do it—"Yes, I'll stay in bed; no, I won't smoke for at least ten days; yes, avoid alcohol—you bet; certainly, I'll come see you if there are any recurrences of the headaches." He anticipated there wouldn't be, since he was still taking medication. He had checked; it was alcohol compatible. And a drink was what he very much wanted. He checked the Rolex—it was three in the afternoon. "Isn't this kind of early for dinner?" Frost asked Bess as she helped him from the car.

"Mary figured a few drinks, then an early dinner, then talking afterward—maybe to sort this thing through."

"I'm for that." Frost nodded, feeling slightly tired after climbing out of the car. "Anything that can shed a little light on these creeps is fine with me."

"You sound like O'Hara—first thing I know you'll be carrying one of those big guns like he does—"

"A .44 Magnum—maybe someday. Ohh—hey—"

"He's got your gun—he's bringing it."

Frost nodded, letting Bess partially support him as he started up the steps.

93

The front door opened; a woman—he recognized her as Mary Boles—came outside, half-running down the steps, holding up an ankle-length skirt with her left hand.

"Captain Frost. I only remember the eye patch. You don't look—"

"I'm not well." Frost nodded. "But I'm O.K."

She got on his left side, to help Bess assist him up the steps.

"Are you sure you should be out of the hospital?"

"No—but the doctors weren't sure either. We decided to gamble." He laughed. "How are you doing?"

"Just a bump on the head." She smiled, as they reached the top of the steps. "But I'm fine otherwise."

"Good," Frost told her, catching his breath, then starting toward the door, Bess and Mary Boles still helping him.

"Here," Mary Boles said as they passed into the entrance hall. "Why don't we go into the library? I can get you some tea."

"Not to be crude," Frost said, "but I'd rather have something a little more—ahh—"

"The bar's in there as well—one of the bars. My family owns this house—I use it though. They live in Europe."

"This is a big place for one woman to take care of," Bess commented, helping Frost to ease into a large, overstuffed chair by the dormant fireplace.

"I know." Mary Boles smiled. "I don't think I could begin to take care of it by myself, but there's a woman who comes to help twice a week—lets herself in if I'm out of town or away on business."

"Just what did you do for Dr. Wells?" Frost asked her, leaning back, lighting a cigarette. Bess brought a pedestal ashtray and put it beside him.

"I was his research assistant."

Frost could feel his heart rate quicken. "Research—then—"

"I already asked her that, Frost," Bess said, sitting on the arm of the chair in which he sat.

"Yes," Mary said, starting across the room toward the built-in paneled bar; bookshelves surrounded it as they did everything else in the room. "And I'll tell you the same thing I told Bess: I just don't know what he was talking about with some terrorist group. It could have been the satanic cultists— What would you like to drink, Captain Frost?"

"Hank— I guess I could use the blood sugar. Make it a screwdriver if you've got orange juice."

"Screwdriver it is." She nodded, turning to the small bar refrigerator beside her. "Plenty here and more in the kitchen. Smirnoff One Hundred do?"

"What I prefer," he told her. "What about the cultists?"

"I've been over this. I'm going to get rid of my purse," Bess said, easing off the arm of the chair and starting across the room. "May I use—?"

"You remember?" Mary Boles asked.

Bess just nodded and left the room.

Frost shook his head, to clear it as Mary Boles brought him his drink. He sipped at it—it was perfect. "Can I get you anything else, Hank?"

"Just what about the satanic cult?"

She sat on the floor a yard or so from his feet, pulling her skirt around her, then studying her hands before she spoke. "The satanic cultists—well, basically, whether or not real satanic blood fetishists exist to any great degree in the United States and Canada is still a mystery. Some evidence indicates they do, but some of the evidence is too preposterous to be believed. The numbers—"

"What do you mean?"

"Well—some professionals estimate that several thousand murders a year are attributable to them, that in some areas whole towns belong to the same cult, and in that way they shroud their activities in secrecy. You know—the sheriff, the newspaper editor—maybe the local clergyman even— I can't speak with any authority there because it's too preposterous."

"But what about these guys?"

"That's the thing. Even if the most gross figures are correct, and there are blood cults operating today— still— Well, it's just hard to imagine an organized group doing what these people have done. It's—"

Frost heard the sound of tires in the driveway, then a car door shutting.

"That must be Mr. O'Hara." Mary Boles smiled, getting to her feet and starting across the room.

Frost sipped at his drink. He had decided that drinking slowly and drinking something with Vitamin C in it would be more sensible than indulging in harder liquor. Anyway, he smiled, he liked orange juice.

He heard the door in the hallway open, then O'Hara's voice. "Well, Miss Boles— That's Frost's rented heap out there, isn't it? Beat me here, huh?"

"You got my gun, O'Hara?" Frost called out from his chair.

Then O'Hara framed himself in the library doorway, a battered attachè case in his right fist. "Yeah—I got it. Dinky little thing. I even cleaned it for you."

"Good." Frost nodded.

"Mike!" It was Bess, her hair looking recombed, a smile on her face as she leaned up and kissed O'Hara on the cheek. "I'm glad you're here. Help me with Frost next time he has to get up some steps." She laughed.

"You feelin' crappy, sport?" O'Hara asked.

"A little." Frost nodded. "But gee, now that you're here—"

"Aww, shut up." O'Hara laughed, setting down the briefcase.

"Can I get you a drink, Mr. O'Hara?"

"I'd love one. Last time I was on duty, this time I'm not," O'Hara answered, following Mary Boles toward the bar. "Some of that Myers dark rum—I always drink it."

"Fine." The woman smiled.

Frost noticed Bess smile, then wink at him. Frost shrugged—was Mike O'Hara romantically turned on? Frost didn't really care; it was O'Hara's business. But from the look on Mary Boles' face, she obviously seemed to care.

"And the first name is Mike," O'Hara told her.

"Call me Mary, then." Mary Boles smiled.

"Getting warm isn't it," Frost whispered to Bess as she again sat beside him on the arm of the overstuffed chair.

She leaned down and kissed his forehead. "It'd be nice if Mike—"

"I know," Frost whispered to Bess. "We could have a double wedding."

"Kill-joy," Bess told him.

"Well," O'Hara began, downing part of his drink. "Aren't you ladies drinking?"

"I'll have scotch, Mary—if you're tending bar."

"That sounds good," Mary Boles answered her. She fixed the drinks, then started across the room.

"Now," Frost asked as she sat down on a rocking chair opposite him and across the front of the fireplace. "What is so strange about these Satanists?"

"M.O.," O'Hara answered for her. "These guys work like the mob—not a bunch of devil-worshipers. That's for openers."

"Mr. O'Hara—ahh—Mike. Well, he's right," Mary Boles began. "These people don't act like true Satanists."

"How would you define a true Satanist, Mary?" Bess asked.

"Well, a true Satanist is very much like a true believer in any religion—in one respect. He or she really believes that his religion is the ultimate expression of his life—at least spiritually. A real Satanist isn't anything like a witch—"

"You mean like the people we saw the night Blanche Corrigan was shot," O'Hara interjected.

"That's right. I understand you were to go to a black mass and that's where poor Blanche was killed. But— Well, that really wasn't a black mass. It could give you some ideas, but—"

"But what?" Bess asked.

"A true black mass is just that: everything in Christianity turned upside down—to the dark side of the spirit world. They worship Satan as their god, and sometimes other satanic deities, much like saints would be worshiped in the Christian context. For example, Astarte—she's the goddess of lust and sexuality."

"Sounds nice." Frost laughed.

"But she isn't—none of them are," Mary Boles answered, visibly trembling. "If real Satanists are at work, they're killers. Anything they did to Dr. Wells, or tried doing . . . well, it's nothing compared to their religious ceremonies."

"Don't follow ya," O'Hara murmured through a sip of rum.

"All right—I'll start again," Mary Boles went on. "You see, there are some who worship Satan as a god. But they aren't really classic Satanists. But if these people are classic Satanists, then there's no way of escaping the violence of what they do. They eat human flesh, drink blood—"

"What?" O'Hara started to cough, choking on his drink.

Frost wanted to laugh, but couldn't somehow. "Drink blood . . . for real? Eat people?"

"Children—or virgins. See, they mimic Christian religious practice, but all for evil. Where part of a Christian ceremony might be the celebration of Communion with the symbolic consumption of bread and wine as the body and blood of Christ—"

"In the Catholic church we don't consider it symbolic," O'Hara said eruditely. "I forget what it's called, but we believe that it actually changes."

"Chief difference from Protestantism," Bess added.

"But for the true Satanist," Mary Boles went on, "they actually use defiled human blood and flesh. They have one thing that they used to do—almost too disgusting to talk about. It involved something called the 'magic cake'—a special kind of black millet—"

"Millet?" Frost asked.

"A grain," Bess told him absently.

"They mixed it sometimes with the ground-up flesh of unbaptized human infants and all ate of it—a sort of perverted communion. And their wine was usually laced with aphrodisiacs—in today's context probably drugs, hallucinogens, psychodeinhibiters."

"Sound like a bunch of lovely people," O'Hara noted sarcastically.

"They have altars," Mary Boles went on. "But rather than draping the altar with clean linen, they usually have a naked woman lie across the altar and they use her abdomen as the table for performing their rites. She stretches out her body like a cross, with her hands out at her sides, and in each hand she holds a black candle."

"That's insane," Frost commented.

"That's mild compared to what they used to do. It's almost indescribably depraved."

"So you think Doc Wells—maybe he knew there was some kind of an outfit like these suckers runnin' around," O'Hara began thoughtfully. "And he figured these guys were like terrorists?"

Frost closed his eye, thinking, not listening to the conversation for a moment; then he opened his eye and downed part of his drink. "What if—" He interrupted Mary Boles. "What if some terrorist group used Satanism as a cover, and used the Satanists to do their dirty work? That would account for somebody just plain shooting Blanche Corrigan, and all those turkeys with the swords. Those fire bombs—they had to have a timing mechanism on the one that exploded inside the elevator shaft. Getting into that building had to be tough—maybe not for professionals, but for amateurs. What if somebody is controlling a bunch of homicidal devil-worshipers—using them?"

"I can't—" Bess started, then shook her head.

"How would anyone use a cult though?" Mary Boles asked, apparently thinking out loud. "The leader of the cult is a priest—another difference from witchcraft. Usually they have women who preside at their ceremonies. But the priest is a male, someone who is the focal point of the cult. In every respect, he's its real leader."

"What if you got some leader with an ax to grind—maybe terrorism, maybe somethin' else?" O'Hara conjectured.

"Somebody using the power of the devil," Bess murmured.

Frost reached out and held her hand tightly, saying, "Don't you worry. The only power of the devil is what people have in their minds. Like I said, these people

100

fall when you shoot 'em."

Bess smiled, but only faintly; her eyes looked worried to Frost as he studied her face.

"Hey," O'Hara interrupted. "If these guys are real Satanists, then there should be whole piles of bodies around from the people they sacrifice—right?"

"No—not necessarily," Mary Boles said. "I doubt any satanic cult today would use infants—just too unavailable. Older children, possibly. There are thousands who disappear each year without a trace. But more likely, they probably use teenage runaways—just pick them up as hitchhikers—"

"Slip 'em drugs—and they wake up getting carved to pieces," O'Hara added.

"And then they dispose of the bodies?" Frost asked.

"Burning—probably that, then scatter the ashes and bones in rivers and abandoned wooded areas. That would give them an unending supply of victims for their rites." Frost lit a cigarette as Mary Boles continued. "They could use virgins just as well as children—to some cultures, a woman doesn't reach adulthood until she's no longer a virgin."

"Where are they gonna find a teenage hitchhiker who's a virgin these days?" O'Hara laughed.

"Mike," Bess chided.

"Sorry, kid." O'Hara smiled. Then he looked at Mary Boles. "But Mary—with all these bodies lying around—well, you'd think that—"

"But they're not lying around," Frost interrupted. "They eat parts of them, then burn them—yuch—and this is an awfully big country. Plenty of places to ditch bodies and with all those things done to them even if some of the remains were recovered, tracing them back, maybe even determining the cause of death would be impossible."

"This sounds like a cheap horror movie," O'Hara

offered.

"Not cheap," Frost commented. "Those Satanists use a lot of extras."

Mary Boles turned out to be a marvelous cook, Frost decided, and he noticed that O'Hara for all his tough talk ate very little of the barbecued ribs. They were beef ribs—Frost had noticed Bess ascertaining that before beginning to eat. Although he sometimes forgot about the differences in their religious backgrounds—meager though his was—he rather respected her for never eating pork because her religion forbade it.

As he wiped off his fingers, the barbecue sauce looking very much like blood, Frost noticed O'Hara. He stared almost transfixedly at the pile of bones at the side of Frost's plate. "Mike? Mike?"

"What?" O'Hara shook his head, looking up.

"These are just—"

"I know—I know," O'Hara snapped. "I was just thinking about somethin' else, that's all."

"Ohh." Frost smiled.

"If you'd like to have your coffee in the library, there's something on television in five minutes or so that should interest you," Mary Boles said. "Especially you." She nodded to Bess.

"You—you mean Dr. Kulley?"

"The topic of his sermon is dealing with Satanism." Mary Boles stood up. O'Hara jumped to his feet. Frost did the same—but more slowly—Bess rising beside him.

"Mike, why don't you help Frost into the library? I'll help Mary with the table," Bess suggested.

"Fine." O'Hara nodded.

"So help already," Frost said, standing there, waiting for O'Hara.

"I hope you trip," O'Hara murmured, walking beside Frost, gingerly taking his elbow.

"I don't think anybody's gonna figure we're goin' together, O'Hara." Frost laughed.

"Look, I'm glad we're alone for a second—gotta talk."

The one-eyed man nodded. They turned out of the dining room, walking slowly down the hallway and into the library.

"Make me a drink, huh?" Frost asked his friend, aiming himself toward the overstuffed chair.

"You want another one of those sissy screwdrivers?"

"Yeah—one sissy screwdriver and hold the mayo," Frost told him, settling himself in the chair and lighting a cigarette. "Now what's so secret and important?"

"This Kulley guy— When you were in the hospital, well, I got Bess dinner last night and she told me about him. You mind?"

"What—that you bought Bess dinner?"

"Well, do you?"

"No," Frost answered. "She's your friend, I know that. And she's my girl; we all know that, too. Should I mind?"

"No, of course not!"

"Then I don't mind. Now, what about Dr. Kulley?"

"Well," O'Hara downed part of a glass of Myers rum as he brought Frost over a screwdriver. "Well, Bess told me about him. And I got to thinking. If these Satanist creeps went after Dr. Wells, and then his secretary, then Mary Boles and Bess and you . . . well . . . why haven't they gone after Lassiter Kulley?"

"Too much of a big shot," Frost said off the top of his head, shrugging his shoulders. "Maybe they just don't take him seriously."

"Look—Mary Boles here—she's refused police protection, says it wouldn't do any good. I know you better than to ask, you aren't gonna want it either."

"So—you gonna go peddle police protection to Dr. Kulley?"

"Yeah—I'm thinkin' about it. Maybe get a few answers, too. If he knows so much about Satanists, maybe he can help us."

Jokingly, Frost said, "What if he's one—a Satanist?"

"Hey! He's a minister," O'Hara said sincerely. "He wouldn't do that!"

"I'm just pullin' your leg," Frost told him.

"But seriously, they're gonna come after you and Bess—that's the primary reason I hung out with her last night until after midnight; then I put some friends in Atlanta P.D. on it informally—just keepin' an eye on her place—the hotel. These Satanists mean business."

"We'll all be fine. They've tried a couple times—haven't gotten me yet."

"I don't think your old bones there are gonna take much more in the way of fires and sword fights, Frost. So you wanna help?"

"Sure." The one-eyed man nodded, inhaling on his cigarette. "What?"

"I already set it up with Bess, I don't guess she told ya yet. I'm gonna push for Mary Boles to take police protection, then Bess is gonna talk her into you guys stayin' here with her to keep an eye on her. Now I got cops down the road, outa sight, the whole nine yards. But if somebody got into the house—well—"

"You mean you wanna throw all three chunks of live bait into the same pond—right?"

"Well, if those Satanist guys could pick one thing they couldn't pass up, it'd be all three of you together.

You game?"

Frost exhaled hard, stubbing out his cigarette. "Yeah. You got more than my Browning in that briefcase?"

"All your spare mags, your knife, that KG-99 thingamabob—"

"I call it an assault pistol."

"Looks like a squirt gun, but it fires semiauto only. Whatever it is—I got that, too. You want somethin' else. How about one of these?" O'Hara reached under his coat, producing the six-inch Magna-Na-Ported, Metalifed Model 29 Smith & Wesson revolver he habitually carried. "You smoke one of them Satan-worshipin' jerks with this baby and they're gone for good—not like that little puny 9mm you use."

"Look—for you that's perfect. For me—I like the Browning, sometimes a .45, but most of the time the Browning. 9mm does just fine for me, see. I don't worry about knockin' guys down with the sound waves when I shoot at 'em. I practiced a lot so I could hit what I shoot at. That's what you're supposed to do with a gun."

"Stop the smart cracks," O'Hara said, holstering his gun under his coat. "So if Bess can swing it—"

"Yeah. If Bess can swing it, I'll do it. Then I can fight whole bunches of those guys at once instead of just three or four at a time. I love it." Frost smiled.

"Hey!" O'Hara looked up; Frost looked around. It was Mary Boles, carrying a tray with coffee cups and other related items on it, coming through the library doors, Bess behind her, carrying a coffee pot. "Dr. Kulley should have started already."

Bess looked at O'Hara, then at Frost; then she told Mary Boles, "They were probably talking guns—that's all they ever do when they get left alone."

"That dame reads ya like a book for the visually impaired, Frost." O'Hara laughed.

Frost said nothing, just nodded.

"I'll get the set," Bess volunteered, going over to it and turning it on. The screen stayed black for an instant, then a face appeared from the middle of it, almost as if it had been planned that way.

Frost recognized the face—from newspapers, magazine articles, television news broadcasts. It was Dr. Lassiter Kulley.

". . . the incarnate evil of the serpent. This same evil which succored man to sin in the garden waits today, to steal away the souls of youth, of all who follow its call to evil pleasure. On the mountain, after the Lord God gave unto Moses His ten commandments, He admonished Moses that death should be brought to all witches—witches, those who practice a religion to the Evil One, the Ape of God whose foul rites are—"

O'Hara reached over and turned down the sound.

"What's he saying?" he asked Mary Boles.

"I think he's saying that Satanism is so evil, satanic cultists and witches, too, should be killed."

"Witches, too—what—"

Bess interrupted him. "Mike, the witches aren't Satanists, remember? They worship the force of nature. But he's tying witches in with satanic cultists."

"Turn up the sound again," Frost told O'Hara.

"I was afraid you were gonna say that," O'Hara groused.

". . . for those who make covenants with witches and Satanists. Saul greatly feared the army of the Philistines, and to know the outcome of battle he sent forth his servant to find a medium, one who could summon the dead from their graves. Disguised—ashamed—he went to the witch of Endor and bade her to summon back Samuel from the grave. And Samuel

106

spake unto Saul that Saul should die, and that his sons should die as well for he had violated God's law: Thou shalt not suffer a witch to live! And Saul, when the battle came and went against him, fell upon his sword, and his head was smote from his body, and his body and those of his sons were displayed for all to see, for such is the fate of those who consort with evil.

"And have we learned, brothers and sisters? Have we learned from this? Do we not still violate God's law? For it is not enough to praise the Lord and then turn away from the evil of Satanism. Those who know of the Evil One's works and do not raise their hands against him are as guilty as those who raise hands to help him perpetrate his unspeakable acts of sacrilege. For God's word is, 'Thou shalt not suffer a witch to live!' And has God's mind changed since those days? Has he become more moderate, more modern, more tolerant of evil personified?

"I say not! Witness the unspeakable death of the well-known panderer to Satan, Dr. Julian Wells! He glorified Satan in his writings, preached tolerance for witches and demons; and they themselves, when they had used him sufficiently to their foul purposes, caused him to die!

"The forces of Satan are everywhere, and as Christians it is our duty—our charge from God—to smite them, to strike them down, to not suffer them to live!"

Applause drowned out Kulley's voice as he cleared his throat—applause and shouts from the audience in the packed hall, shouts of "Amen!" and "Hallelujah!"

The camera cut to a commercial and O'Hara shut off the television.

Frost realized he had a coffee cup in his hand and the coffee was cold. Bess took it from him, spilling half of it into the saucer. "People like that scare me," she

107

murmured. "He's not saying anything evil himself, he's saying we should fight evil—and that's good. But there's something about the way he says it."

"You mean just follow me, guys, and turn off your brains?"

"I can't see a legitimate religious person saying what he says," O'Hara offered.

"He was like that in the interview—a little of the Bible, a lot of fundamentalist politics and preaching violence—really. He's amazing," Bess said, looking stunned.

"This guy's real popular, I understand," O'Hara said half-heartedly.

"Look," Mary Boles said, her voice too cheerful sounding. "Look—if anyone should be upset it should be me. Dr. Wells was probably a better Christian than Dr. Kulley could ever be. But yet Dr. Kulley is calling Julian a pawn of the devil. You can't let someone like Dr. Kulley get under your skin."

"Well, I tell ya somethin', Mary," O'Hara began, looking at the floor in front of his feet, then suddenly looking up toward her face. "If I were one of those Satanist guys? I'd smoke Kulley and fast. 'Cause what that guy was just saying is to go out and kill somebody you think talks to the devil or communicates with the dead or any of that garbage. He's tellin' people it's God's law that they murder other people."

"They did that already," Frost told O'Hara, lighting a cigarette. "They called it the Inquisition." Frost smiled as he inhaled the cigarette smoke into his lungs. Sometimes he was very glad he didn't think he was "good"—whatever that was.

Chapter Eleven

Frost spent most of the next three days sleeping on the couch at the far end of the library. Mary Boles and Bess were working at the other end of the library, pouring over research notes made by Dr. Wells—his books, his business records, these latter gotten as copies from his accountant. While Frost rested, the two women worked, trying to determine what Julian Wells had meant by a terrorist group and what specifically the nature of the satanic blood cult could be. When Frost would stir in his sleep he would roll over at times and open his eye to see that the two women were safe and that the Metalifed High Power still hung in the Cobra shoulder rig on the chair a few feet from the couch—ready if the police Mary Boles hadn't wanted guarding her accidentally let someone through down the private road to her house, ready if the Satanists tried again, as the one-eyed man knew they would.

On the afternoon of the third day, feeling fitter and finally through with the course of antibiotics he had been taking, Frost left the house. A chill was in the air, compounded by the fact he hadn't been outside in days. Over his shoulder rig, he wore a windbreaker.

He walked the grounds, trying to determine what types of flowers grew along the driveway up from the road, watching the patterns of the clouds as they scudded on the wind—in general going mad with boredom.

He heard the sound of the car before he turned around and saw it. It was a U.S. Government car. The car stopped a few feet from the portico in front of the house and Mike O'Hara climbed out. He waved and started toward Frost. Frost, suddenly happy to see O'Hara—he would have been happy to see anyone—started toward the car.

They met at the edge of the portico farthest from the house.

"Well— You believe no news is good news?" O'Hara grinned.

"Not particularly," Frost told him.

"Then I don't have good news."

"Nothing from Dr. Kulley?"

"He says he's been threated by satanic groups and bunches of other people over the years—but no one's ever followed through. He doesn't worry about these creeps, but he said that just to make me feel better, he'd increase his security."

"What kinda setup's he got?" Frost asked, lighting a cigarette. He didn't wait for O'Hara to answer. "Come on—let's take a walk."

"But keep the house in sight, right?"

"Always." Frost laughed. "So—what kinda setup's he got?"

"Guys with automatic weapons—all legal. Figured it would be. Guard dogs—I was almost afraid to get out of my car. He doesn't live poor, Dr. Kulley. I didn't ask what the estate he lives on was worth; I already knew—checked it out. Owned by 'Kulley Enterprises,' nonprofit, religious. About a million and a half bucks. And I also did some more checking on this Martin fella that keeps turning up. Even showed Kulley the Identi-Kit picture—never heard of the guy. I figured that. Still nothing on any of those satanic cultists that you got into it with. Nothing at all. But

110

there's something real interesting; the lab lost the ballistics report on Blanche Corrigan, and the bullet they took out of her head temporarily has been misplaced. So all we know about the bullet is that it came from a gun like a couple thousand others. You know how many cops alone use Model 59s? Just here in the U.S. And it's a popular gun with civilians, too. But the lab doesn't usually lose records like that—you know what I mean?"

"More of the Martin whitewash I got when he killed my old C.O. in 'Nam?"

"Maybe," O'Hara said. "Just maybe. And they pulled me off the case for a while till we get somethin' fresh."

"Off the case?" Frost repeated, dropping his cigarette and heeling it out on the ground.

"Well, I don't think really that's phony or anything. There's been a big thing brewin' for the last year and a half or so. Kidnapping—Dr. Ronald Paulson, big agriscientist doin' top-secret work for the government. So secret they won't even tell me why the Ruskies might want him. But looks like three other scientists were snatched over the last eighteen months—two men and a woman, all the same field, all the same project, but different aspects of it. All of them unofficially have turned up in the Soviet Union. So— Well, I gotta work on this kidnap thing. More important than a bunch of Satanists they tell me, and there's still no definite ruling as to whether or not FBI has jurisdiction with the Satanist thing anyway. Might not."

"So—local police?"

"Yeah, they got it." O'Hara smiled. "But they're good guys, and as soon as something pops on this, I'll be back on, come hell or high water."

"It's the hell part I'm afraid of," Frost told him, lighting another cigarette.

111

"Figured I'd come and tell ya in person—rather than just usin' the horn."

"I appreciate it," Frost told his friend.

"Say hello to Bess, huh? I gotta run."

"Walk you back to the car," Frost told him. If Martin was part of a cover-up, what possible connection could there have been between the years-old assassination of his C.O. in Vietnam and a satanic cult? The one-eyed man just shook his head, afraid he was going to find out, like it or not. . . .

"Perfect night for a ghost story, isn't it?" Frost said to Bess, his arm around her as they stood on the front porch. The moon was bright in the sky and the wind blew the clouds along; it was cool. He had learned that in the old house when the wind blew from just the right direction, you could hear it whistle through cracked boards, the whistling sound almost like a sigh. It was that way tonight.

He felt Bess shiver beside him. "Let's go inside." She smiled up at him.

"Buy ya a drink," he told her. "Or I guess Mary Boles will."

"Too bad she was so tired," Bess murmured absently as they walked inside.

"The way you guys have been going through Dr. Wells's things, I'm surprised either one of you can see straight." Frost laughed. "Besides—she's looked bushed for the last couple of days—probably needs the rest."

"You feeling better?" Bess asked him, pushing the front door closed behind her, leaning against it a moment with her hands behind her back.

"Yeah. Back among the living again. Wouldn't wanna run the hundred for a while, but I'm fine."

"When will they come after us?"

Frost shrugged, lighting a cigarette in the blue-yellow flame of his Zippo. The wind, keening from outside, was more audible than he would have liked on the inside. "Soon—I think. Maybe they won't come back at all."

"You want them to, don't you?" Bess asked him.

"Fix me that drink," he told her, leaning over to her and kissing her lightly on the lips. "And yeah, they've gotta come back. That's the only way we'll ever get them. You know that."

"But we're not the police."

"You want Wells's murderer just as badly as I do," Frost told her.

"But I guess I don't want to get killed finding him."

"We won't get killed—promise." He smiled. "Now, how about that drink?"

He had one scotch and half of another before looking at his Rolex. It was just a few minutes after midnight and he watched the date changing. "You wanna go to bed?" he asked her, sitting alone with her in the library.

"I should go through the notes for Dr. Wells's latest book. It wasn't finished. I told Mary Boles I might help her finish it. She isn't a writer—just a researcher in the occult. Kind of important to her that the book gets out. It was the last thing he worked on before his death," Bess said quietly.

"Kiss of death on it?"

"Maybe," Bess answered.

"Just makes you want to do it all the more, doesn't it?"

"Uh-huh." She smiled.

"I know," Frost told her. "You're the same as I am. If a news story was easy to get, you wouldn't want it. If nobody was holding onto a hill like his life depended on it, I wouldn't be charging up the hill trying to take

113

it."

"Any hope for us?" She laughed, taking a swallow of her drink.

"One of these days," he told her. "One of these days. Come on—let's make love."

"You talked me into it," she said, not looking at him, but studying the drink in her hands instead. "Frost?"

"What?"

"I mean— Well, we don't get a chance to, to be in a house like this with a stairway like that." She gestured toward the hallway.

The stairway to the second floor looked like something out of a movie set, slightly arcing, red carpeted, wide.

Frost dropped his voice. "Frankly my dear—"

"Ohh, shut up." She laughed.

Walking around behind the bar, Frost took Bess into his arms, kissing her hard on the mouth, pulling her body close against his, bending it against the contours of his own.

"All right," he whispered into her left ear. "I'll carry you. After all, this is Georgia and you gotta say," he added, the howling in the rafters louder now, "we've got plenty of wind. Haven't we?"

Frost swept her up into his arms. It always looked easier when you watched someone else do it, in a movie, he thought. Adult women, especially ones of average height or better, could be heavy. All of this, plus the fact that his shoulders already ached, came to Frost as he stood at the base of the stairs.

"Can you make it, Frost?"

He looked down into her eyes. "I hope you studied CPR somewhere along the line—just in case I get a heart attack." She laughed, and Frost bent his head over her and kissed her, resettling her where she was

114

cradled in his arms, then starting up with her.

There were twenty-four stairs by the time he reached the wide, pie-shaped stair that was like a small landing. He resettled her in his arms, Bess laughing now; then he tackled the remaining stairs—another twelve.

He reached the top, panting, his shoulders aching even more. "You want me to walk the rest of the way?" she murmured softly.

"No. Hell, I'm enjoying this," he told her, walking—heavily—toward their bedroom door as Bess hit the downstairs hall-light switch. The only light below them was from the aquarium—Mary Boles raised tropical fish—in the rear of the main hall. From the aquarium a greenish light emanated down the hallway and across the first floor.

Frost stopped outside their bedroom door. "I can walk from here," Bess told him.

"Naw—don't worry." He smiled, fumbling at the doorknob. It wouldn't open. He tried again, finally twisting it and pushing inward. The door opened, he started through. Bess groaned and he realized he'd slammed her ankles into the doorjamb. "Sorry, kid." He smiled. He turned sideways, then took her through the door. Bess hit the upstairs hall-light switch just outside their door and now they were in near-total darkness. He kicked the door closed gently behind them, only the light of the moon which shone through the windows relieving the blackness. Above his own labored breathing, he could hear the wind in the eaves of the old house.

He walked over beside the bed, barking his shins against its heavy lower frame. He set Bess on the bed, almost collapsing beside her. "Not as young as you used to be," she whispered in his left ear.

"Wanna bet?" Frost answered, leaning over her,

crushing his mouth down on hers, his right hand edging up under the hem of her dress, moving along her thigh, pressing against the fabric of the panties she wore under it.

Her arms circled his neck, her fingers touched his skin, her breath was hot against him as he bent his head to kiss her neck. His hand had found the top of her panties and was starting to pull them down. She moved beside him on the bed, her legs spreading and her dress and slip bunching up toward her hips.

He started to pull her panties down as she raised herself up so he could.

But he stopped just below her triangle of hair, his fingers exploring it, kneading it, feeling the moisture and the warmth there.

"Make love to me," she murmured.

"What do you think I'm doing?" he told her.

She laughed, holding him more tightly as his fingers searched her, explored her. "I can get my dress off—if you help," she whispered.

Frost reached behind her, finding the zipper. She sat up as he undid the little hook and eye at the top, then pulled the zipper down the length of her back. The dress was gray, like the meager light; it made the whiteness of her back and the whiteness of the bra even whiter. He helped her as she pulled the dress over her head; then he undid the bra. She slipped it off her right shoulder, letting the left strap hang in the crook of her left elbow. He bent over her, kissing the erect nipples of her breasts.

"Here," she murmured, reaching up to him. He shrugged out of his sportcoat, then the shoulder rig. He let both go to the floor.

He could feel her hands unbuttoning his shirt; then her fingers pressing against his chest, her nails twisting in the hair there. He undid the buttons of his cuffs,

116

then let her slip the shirt off.

He could feel her hands fumbling with his belt, then his trousers, pulling the zipper down. He leaned back across the bed as she pulled his pants off, felt her lips touch his thighs, her hands rubbing at him through his underpants. She started pulling them off; Frost's fingers kneaded her breasts.

"What's that?" She laughed, grabbing at him.

"You'll find out in a minute," he told her. He pulled her panties down all the way, throwing them to the floor, pushing her slip up to her waist, sliding between her thighs. He could feel the nylon stockings she wore—they somehow magically held themselves up at her thighs—then above them, against his own skin, the flesh of her thighs. They were warm.

He pressed himself harder against her, her hands guiding him as he entered her. She shuddered, holding her arms wrapped tight around him, her body arching up under his, pressing against him.

"Are you in a hurry?" she half-whispered, half-gasped.

"No," he told her, and she held him more tightly. . . .

Frost opened his eye; Bess was saying something to him. "Wake up, Frost—I hear something."

He tried rolling over, but his left arm was still around her. He rolled over toward her instead and glanced at the luminous face of the Rolex in the darkness. It was two A.M. "There's nobody downstairs except the fish in the aquarium," he told her, hugging her close to him, kssing her lightly on the mouth, then closing his eye.

"Frost! I hear something!"

He heard something, too—but it was the wind in the eaves. "The wind," he whispered, trying not to talk loudly so he wouldn't awaken fully.

"It's not the wind. Do you want me to get up and look?"

"Bess," he groaned. "It's the wind."

"Shh—listen—"

Frost heard a thudding sound, then nothing. "Just a loose board—this house is full of 'em—go to sleep. I'll take care of you." He held her tightly again, then closed his eye.

"Frost!"

He opened his eye, then sat bolt upright. "All right. If it'll make you feel better, I'll go wander around and have a look. O.K.?"

"O.K." she smiled in the pale moonlight.

He threw his legs over the side of the bed and sat there a moment, rubbing his eye. "Shit," he murmured.

"What?"

"Nothing," he told her. He found his eye patch and pulled it on, then went to the foot of the bed. Finding his shoulder rig, he pulled the Metalifed High Power from it.

At the foot of the bed, he sat, trying to untangle his trouser legs. "You still don't own a bathrobe?"

"I had one—can't remember what the hell happened to it," he told her. He stood up, zipping his pants. "Ouch," he cursed.

"What's the matter?"

"Ahh—forgot I wasn't wearing underpants— caught the hair on my crotch in the zipper." He tugged the zipper free, along with a few hairs, then closed his pants and buckled his belt. He stuffed the High Power into his trouser band, the metal cold against his skin.

Barefoot, he started for the door. "If you're worried, lock the door after me," he told her. "Be back in

118

a minute. Want a glass of milk or anything?"

"No. Just be careful. I'm sure I—"

"Hey. It's all right. I love you," he told her, forcing a smile which he realized she couldn't see anyway in the poor light.

He opened the door, listening, hearing nothing except the hum of the aquarium machinery and the wind. He shrugged, yawning, then stepped through into the hallway. A glow of light came from the base of the stairs—the aquarium. He closed the door, heard Bess lock it behind him, then started down the hallway toward the head of the stairs.

He waited there for a moment, hearing nothing.

He shrugged again, yawned again, and sat down on the top stair, listening. His lighter was in his trouser pocket, but he'd left his cigarettes. "Nuts," he murmured. He stood up, then slowly—he was tired, still half-asleep—he started down the stairs, toward the first floor.

The glow was stronger there from the aquarium, its greenish tinge more predominant.

He stopped midway, on the pie-wedge-shaped stair, listening. He heard nothing new, nothing odd. He kept walking. He reached the base of the stairs and stopped.

His right hand flashed to the Metalifed High Power as he wheeled.

Something came at him out of the wash of green aquarium light, dark, indistinct.

He jacked back the hammer of the High Power, simultaneously dodging a flash of metal cutting at him out of the darkness. His right fist balled on the butt of the pistol, the first finger of his right hand starting the squeeze, as the sword blade flashed down and past him.

There was a whooshing sound and Frost edged

away from it. Something thudded down across his right forearm, numbing it, the gun falling from his hand and hitting the floor. He started to stumble backward, against the stairs, the whooshing sound coming again.

Frost looked to his right. A spiked ball, and leading from the end of it a chain, held by something that looked like a night stick but was attached to the other end of the chain.

He couldn't remember what you called it as he dodged it. The spiked ball hammered against the vertical supports for the stair railing, shattering them.

Frost edged back as the sword-wielder stepped into the light—black robed, one of the Satanists. "Listen pal, can't we talk this over?" Frost asked. His gun was lost somewhere on the floor, his right arm stiff; but feeling was returning to it. His left hand touched the skin; his fingers came away bloody. "Great," he murmured, still edging away.

The swordsman was joined by the other robed figure, the one with the heavy ball and chain. Frost edged back, toward the aquarium, its green light brighter now. "Hey, if you're gonna kill me with that thing, at least tell me what it is. I can never remember. A mace or a flail?"

A voice—a woman's—came from the recesses of the black hood. "A flail."

"Thanks, honey." Frost nodded, dodging as the robed woman swung the flail outward and downward. "Flail," Frost repeated, the whooshing sound loud behind him as he dodged left. The flail crashed down against the glass wall of the one hundred-gallon aquarium.

"Boy! Those fish are gonna be mad," the one-eyed man shouted, dropping to his hands, his left leg balancing him, tucked under him as he swept his right leg

120

out, against the legs of the woman with the flail. She stumbled, falling back, into the glass and water of the ruined aquarium.

Frost rolled right, getting wet, feeling glass under his hands as the sword-wielding Satanist started for him. As the man lunged, Frost dodged right, and snatching up the Atlanta yellow pages from the telephone table, heaved it at the swordsman's head. The swordsman dodged; Frost dived for him, headfirst, hammering at the right side of the man's rib cage, then dodging away as the swordsman recovered and hacked with his blade. Frost fell back against the telephone table beside the wall. The woman with the flail was getting to her feet. Her black robe was up past her thighs and Frost decided her legs weren't bad.

Again Frost snatched up the Atlanta white pages, hurtling it at the woman's chest, knocking her off balance. The sword-wielding man was coming again. Frost snatched up the small chair beside the telephone table. He blocked the sword cut with the chair which splintered under its impact. Frost's left foot snapped up into the robed killer's crotch. There was a scream, more animal than human. Frost's right fist locked on the wrist of his assailant's sword hand, his left snapping up and out, inside the man's guard. The heel of his left hand impacted against the base of the man's nose, breaking the bone, bringing it up into the brain. The robed assassin died before he fell.

Frost grabbed the sword; the woman with the flail came for him. As the one-eyed man raised the sword, the flail half-wrapped around its blade. He jerked the sword up and back, pulling the woman off balance. His left fist crashed across her jaw; her head snapped hard against the wall as she sprawled toward it, then sank into the mess of glass, water, and dying tropical fish on the floor.

121

Frost started back up the hall, for his gun. He reached into the shadow outside the greenish light that topped the otherwise-destroyed aquarium. The gun was gone. He heard a laugh and stepped back, startled, as a slicing sound filled the air. It was another swordsman, the sword moving in his hands like a living entity, searching for Frost's blood. Raising his sword as the swordsman made his lunge, Frost backstepped. He blocked the move, recovered, blocked another downward hack; then he twisted the blade in his hands to block a lateral slice. The swordsman laughed again, and from the darkness on the second floor above him, Frost could hear a scream—Bess.

"Frost! Frost!"

The one-eyed man dived left, into the hall near the door, rolling, but awkwardly because he held the sword. The swordsman laughed again, louder, lunged for him. Frost edged back. A long, narrow Oriental throw rug was on the hallway floor and somewhere, in the back of his mind, Frost remembered an old movie. As the swordsman lunged again, Frost dropped, grabbing at the rug, pulling it hard, tugging it out from under the feet of the swordsman. Then the one-eyed man was up, his own borrowed sword in both his hands, hacking down. The swordsman, still on his back, parried Frost's blade, but Frost hacked again, then again, their blades locking. Then Frost's blade slipped past the guard of the other man, slicing away three fingers. The swordsman dropped his blade and screamed. Frost cleaved the front of his skull in two.

Frost looked around him and seeing no one near, quickly searched the body of the dead swordsman— the High Power.

Frost dropped the magazine, checked the chamber; the gun hadn't been touched.

Replacing the magazine, he took up the sword in his

122

right hand, the pistol in his left, and, racing up the stairs three at a time, shouted, "Bess! I'm coming!"

When he reached the top of the stairs, three robed figures ran toward him.

He pumped the trigger of the Metalifed High Power, twice, then twice again, two of them going down. He parried a thrust from the last of the swordsmen, and, blocking the blade, punched the muzzle of the High Power forward, firing twice point-blank, into the chest and neck of the robed killer.

The body fell back.

Frost started toward a shaft of light at the end of the hallway—not his and Bess's room, but Mary Boles's room.

Frost heard the scream again. "Frost! Stay back!"

He raced toward the light, hacking the blade wildly through the open doorway as he jumped inside. On the bed, Mary Boles was dead, her throat slit ear to ear.

In the corner of the room, Bess stood, her arms held behind her, a robed figure holding what looked like a butcher knife against her throat.

Frost snapped, "Let her go, asshole," then took two steps.

Something thudded against the back of his head and he felt the worst pain there he had ever known.

Chapter Twelve

"Truck," the one-eyed man murmured. "Truck . . ."

"What, Captain Frost?"

"Truck—truck hit me—my head."

"My security people said it appeared to be some sort of club—broke the skin, gave you a nasty bruise, but nothing permanent."

"Truck—not a club," Frost repeated. He opened his eye then, to find out who had been talking with him.

"Kulley. Lassiter Kulley," the now-familiar voice offered.

"Lassiter Kulley. O.K.," Frost murmured, then closed his eye again. . . .

Realizing that he was lying down, on a couch of some kind, he opened his eye once more. His hands moved; so did his feet. He tried to move his head—it ached. "Are you back with us again, Captain Frost?"

"Yeah—I think," he told the voice. He remembered the voice. On television— But he'd heard it before, more recently. "Kulley?"

"That's right. We spoke a little while ago, when you woke up the first time."

Frost sat up, swinging his legs over the side of the— It was a couch. His head screamed at him not to do something foolish like that again, and he held his head in his hands, thinking of a way to apologize to his head for moving it, to cajole it to stop aching.

"Nasty bump on the head, but I think you'll live. Agent O'Hara promised to bring a doctor with him when he arrived."

"O'Hara?" Frost looked up at the name; his head ached more and he regretted it. He buried his face in his hands, then repeated the name, "O'Hara?"

"Your friend. You remember him surely?"

"Yeah. You called Mike?"

"Yes—after my associates found you and Miss Stallman."

"Bess!" He looked up this time, not caring that his head ached. Kulley sat on the edge of a massive and ornate desk across the room, his cordovan wing tip-shod feet dangling in midair, like a child's might. He smiled broadly. "Bess—where?" Then the pain came again.

"She's fine—resting comfortably. Quite honestly, she seemed terrified and I think once she realized you were going to survive—well, sleep was the only thing."

"Where—where is—?"

"Upstairs, using one of the bedrooms. In all candor, I decided to let you stay here in my office out of purely selfish reasons—in the hope that you would awaken before Mr. O'Hara and his FBI associates arrived, and shed some light on what happened."

"Mary Boles—she's—"

"Yes—I know. Throat slit. I'm glad I wasn't there to see it. It just must have been grisly. But what was the last thing you remember happening?"

"Bess," Frost murmured. "She screamed. I ran upstairs, into Mary Boles's room. Saw Mary on the bed—throat cut. Then some asshole in a black robe with a knife at Bess's throat. I went for him, then—ohh," the one-eyed man murmured, suddenly recalling it all. "What—?"

125

"My own security people. After Mr. O'Hara spoke to me, it set me to thinking. Perhaps these were indeed a different breed of satanic cultists. I had my own investigators locate their headquarters, then sent several of my men there to keep them under observation, to be certain these were in fact the ones responsible for the murder of the unfortunate Dr. Wells and the others. Well, almost immediately after my men arrived, they saw a group of the cultists leaving their headquarters, carrying some sort of equipment. One of the cultists dropped something—a suitcase I believe. At any event, a sword clattered out onto the street. My security people contacted me by radio. I advised them to follow the cultists before summoning the police. Police with their sirens, their flashing lights—I think sometimes all that does more to warn off criminals than to apprehend them."

"I don't—"

"I know. This must all be so confusing." Kulley smiled, solicitiously. Frost saw something in the smile that he couldn't quite decide about—did it calm or alarm him? "But my men did follow, to Mary Boles's house. Somehow, just as they arrived, they saw the police leaving. I gather police had been stationed up the road from the house?"

"Yeah—some," Frost told him.

"My men grew suspicious at this, then followed the satanic cultists along the road. They were reluctant to break into the home, as had the Satanists, but finally heard screaming from the house. They went inside in force, killed three of the Satanists, and rescued Miss Stallman and yourself. Unfortunately, the other satanic cultists fled."

"You call the cops?" Frost asked, searching his pants pockets for cigarettes. He still wasn't wearing a shirt.

"I was afraid to contact local police. What if their being called away was part of some sort of conspiracy? What if they were in league with the Satanists?"

"Atlanta cops? Naw," Frost murmured. "But I guess—ohh . . ." His head seemed to vibrate again. "But I guess you did the right thing—calling O'Hara. How soon?"

"I'd say less than an hour. When I told him you weren't seriously hurt and Miss Stallman was well, he apparently wanted to go to Miss Boles' home first, to look for clues, or whatever FBI agents do." Kulley smiled broadly. "Now, sir, are you well enough to perhaps share a cup of coffee with me?"

"Coffee?" Frost looked at his watch. "Yeah—fine." He nodded. He shouldn't have nodded—the pain again. "Fine," he repeated, this time not moving his head.

"Good. I'd like for us to talk a bit, and I know what your head must feel like—had a skiing accident once years ago that gave me a bad knot on the head."

"Yeah—I hurt." Frost smiled. "Hey—thanks, thanks a lot," Frost added.

"My pleasure, sir. I think it's safe to say we're all on the same side, regardless of our motivations—or like the young people say, regardless of where our heads are at. Hmm?" Kulley laughed, half-jumping down from the edge of his desk and walking around behind it to an automatic coffee maker. "I'm afraid I can't offer you anything stronger—my beliefs. Liquor corrupts both body and spirit."

"Coffee's fine." Frost nodded. His head ached. He shouldn't have nodded, he realized.

"You're familiar with my work then?"

"Saw you on television—yeah," Frost told him.

"Do I detect a note of disapproval in your voice?"

"No—not really. My philosophy has always been to

127

live and let live. Yours isn't. That's your prerogative," Frost answered.

"Sounds rather liberal for a man in your profession," Kulley remarked.

Something in what Kulley said bothered Frost; he couldn't put his finger on it. "I'm not a liberal—unless you mean it in the classical sense. I believe in the free interchange of ideas, rights of individuals so long as they don't interfere with anybody else's rights—that sort of thing. But the way you define liberal these days—hell, I'm no liberal."

"Well, although I wouldn't have put it that way, I suppose we're in some sort of philosophical agreement. I'm not a liberal either. Have you and Miss Stallman learned anything about Dr. Wells's investigations—any reason why these satanic cultists would have murdered him?"

"You seemed pretty certain the other day. Who was it you talked about in your sermon?"

"It was Saul." Kulley smiled, handing Frost a cup of black coffee in a tall, truck stop–style white mug. Frost looked at the mug a moment; all that was missing were the cracks. "Actually I oversimplified a little. Saul was rather like you really. A good warrior, but never seemed to be able to do things quite right. And he was good-hearted. God damned him to death not merely because he consulted the witch of Endor, but because he failed to kill all the people of Amalek. He spared their king, Agag. Much as I imagine in your profession that life would be easier if somehow you'd been able over the years to kill all the Communists in the world. But then your philosophy might have gotten in the way. What would you do if you encountered a totally innocent person who just happened to be a Communist, but didn't try to advance his cause, had done you no personal or collective harm—was simply a philosophical Communist? Would you shoot him?"

"No—probably," Frost told Kulley.

"As I said—like Saul to a degree."

"So long as I don't wind up dead like him."

"Most interesting death," Kulley went on. "He realized he was losing a battle and rather than face capture at the hands of the Philistines, he ordered his armorbearer to kill him. The armorbearer wouldn't, so Saul did it himself. It was later that his head was lopped off. Are you the type to fall on your sword?"

"I don't think so," Frost answered. He sipped at the coffee. It seemed exotic—not the ordinary variety. The taste was pleasant, and a bit sweet.

"I don't think so either. Perhaps, despite our differences, we can put our heads together about this satanic cult business. Now—did you ascertain why Dr. Wells was victimized?"

"All I know—and it isn't much," Frost volunteered, "is that Wells was planning to go to the FBI the next morning, with information about some sort of terrorist group that posed a serious threat to U.S. security. Since Satanists killed him, they must have been the group. You should buy that—from your sermon. What more serious threat to security than people who pervert the minds of youth?"

"But I'm certain Dr. Wells had something more concrete."

"Not as far as the notes and materials we went through. Nothing. He was researching the backgrounds of various individual satanic groups and the possibility that there really were blood cultists operating in the United States, linked to mutilation murders, whatever."

"Much as your Miss Stallman is doing."

"Yeah." Frost nodded. He noticed that the pain in his head was subsiding. He sipped at more of the sweet-tasting coffee. "She's trying. But it all seems to be a dead end. Could be, I guess," Frost theorized, "that somebody's using this blood-cult stuff to cover up some sort of operation, maybe terrorists, maybe something else. That might be what Wells had in mind. But unless he had notes someplace else, or we can retrace his steps, we might never know."

"Fascinating." Kulley smiled.

Frost looked at his watch again. The face was a little blurred. He attributed it to the bump on his head. "Let me try raising O'Hara. He should be here. It's four A.M."

"He was very specific—said he'd be here and for us not to contact him again. He mentioned something about security."

"I wanna see Bess," Frost said suddenly. He was feeling odd and didn't know exactly why he'd said it. But it sounded to him like a good idea. "I wanna see Bess," he said again, downing more of the coffee—it would keep him awake and suddenly he felt very tired.

"I'm afraid that's impossible. She's sleeping."

"Then I'll wake her up," Frost answered.

"No." Kulley smiled.

Frost sipped at his coffee—the aftertaste. He tossed the coffee mug down on the white rug at his feet. "This was—"

"Drugged," Kulley interrupted.

"You son of—" Frost started to his feet, lurching awkwardly toward the desk. He saw Kulley push a small buzzer near the telephone.

"Sit down, Captain Frost." Kulley edged away, dodging Frost as Frost reached for him.

Frost started lurching after him; the door opened and Frost wheeled toward it. The one-eyed man dropped to his knees, unable to stand, his vision badly blurred; something like a voice in his head screamed at

130

him.

Through the doorway came a man. The man's face was distorted, but then Frost's vision cleared for an instant.

"Martin!"

Frost saw the pistol crash down toward his head, then he saw nothing else.

Chapter Thirteen

He was naked. He felt the cold stone against his bare skin before the pain returned in his head. "Blind?" He muttered to the darkness, his lips dried and cracked. He could see nothing. And closing his eye, squinting it tight, then opening it again, did nothing. There was still only blackness around him.

He heard a moaning sound. Was it in his head? He remembered the sound just before— "Martin—" he gasped. Martin and Dr. Kulley. But that was impossible. He tried to lick his lips, but the sweet taste of the coffee—he remembered that. The coffee. Drugged. He tried to move. His head reeled, but his hands would not move; nor would his feet. He tried arching his back, but something kept him from doing that. He felt the things now—rope of some kind, on his wrists and his ankles and across his abdomen.

He tugged at the ropes, heard the moaning again. Awake enough to realize it wasn't inside his head, he was also awake enough to realize that all wasn't right in his head. Dizziness. A feeling of being out-of-body. A coldness more than that of the cold stone beneath his skin. And his skin was damp, clammy. He had a nauseated feeling in the pit of his stomach.

He tried to make himself see, closing his eye, counting to ten, then opening his eye again.

There was a grayness now and he thought he could make out the skin of his chest, of his right shoulder.

132

Was it that it was total darkness surrounding him? He asked himself. And why?

He struggled against the ropes binding him, the coarse rope gouging into his flesh as he tugged at it.

He closed his eye, a wave of nausea sweeping over him. His head ached; the taste of the sweet coffee still lingered in his mouth.

He decided to concentrate his effort against his bonds. He began to tug at the rope on his right wrist, using the ropes binding his left wrist as leverage, to loosen them.

The rope abraded his right wrist and he could feel the skin pulling and ripping, but he was able now to twist his right wrist—a little. A wave of nausea washed over him again, and he closed his eye against it.

When he opened his eye, there was a light, far off in the darkness, but a bright light, flickering. Was it his vision? The light seemed to grow in intensity, as did the moaning sound he had been hearing since awakening.

He watched the light, for what seemed like an eternity, lying motionless, the tugging against his bonds forgotten. Pain—his head, his right wrist, the back of his neck, and stiffness in his knees and elbow joints as well. His arms were drawn out, at right angles to his body, his body forming with them— He almost wretched. His legs were drawn straight beneath him, together, the legs making the base, his trunk forming the main timber with them, his arms the cross-members, his head— A cross.

And now he could see the light more clearly, glowing, flickering; and behind it, almost obscured by the brightness of the first light, another, and farther behind that—a pinpoint-sized gold dot—still another light.

The moaning grew louder, and he could distinguish

133

part of a word in it—a chant. The word—he literally prayed he was wrong—was "Satan!"

Chapter Fourteen

Torchlight ringed him now. The bodies of the bearers of the torches were obscured by the shadowy blackness of the robes which enveloped them. No faces were visible either, because the pointed and cowled hoods obscured the shape, the very form of their heads.

The words of the chant were indecipherable to him—Latin, but sounding not quite right. As a boy he had infrequently attended Catholic churches, in the days before the mass had been changed to the vernacular of the host country. But he usually recognized Latin. Somehow though it was as if the Latin words were jumbled, backward, ripped apart and reassembled by a madman.

But the one word he had feared he had heard was now unmistakable. They were chanting to Satan.

"Satani!"

He tugged at the bonds on his wrists, the blood on his chafed right wrist now visible to him in the torchlight.

He felt himself sweating—he lied to himself—from the heat of the torches surrounding him. But inside himself he knew the real reason—fear.

The chant suddenly, inexplicably, changed. A different chant. Still the dominant word "Satani". Still the rhythmic quality. But the rhythm faster now. And in the right hands of the robed figures surrounding him, their left hands holding the torches, he could now see the flicker of knives.

He looked at the figures more closely. Some of them, around their waists, wore belts, and from the belts—studded leather, the buckles ornate and brass colored—were suspended scabbards, and in these were swords, swords like those he had fought against. Dr. Wells. Blanche Corrigan. Mary Boles. Suddenly, sickened, he wondered how many others had died by them—whether the swords themselves were the instruments, or just part of the show. Was this the conspiracy Wells had planned to expose to the FBI?

The circle of robed figures parted, just at the edge of his vision, above his head, and from beyond the circle, as the chant increased in volume and pace once more, he could see movement.

He saw the flash of steel first, a sword, but shorter, the blade ornately carved, and the hands that held it slender. The hands were white, chalky white, like those of a dead person, the fingernails black. The hands led to arms, red streaks like those made from blood poisoning ran the course of the forearms across the chalky whiteness and ended at the elbows. The whiteness suddenly vanished there; a bizarre mixture of red and green and yellow covered the body—naked, a woman's body, the breasts upcurved and firm, the nipples an unnatural and somehow compelling coal black, the coronas around them blood red.

Then he saw the face. Pentagrams, and other marks were emblazoned on the cheeks and forehead. The other marks he didn't understand, their color was black, the face chalky white like the forearms, and the lips black.

She danced, and now as the chant once more increased its rapidity, its intensity, she wove the blade through the air, across his body, less than inches from his face, her left hand snatching at his crotch, stroking

136

him, her black lips curled back in a smile, her teeth blood red.

He watched her, never taking his eye from her, as the blade sliced the air above him. Sweat glistened over the paint on her body; animal moans came from her—like the sounds of an angry cat—assailing his ears.

She swiped the blade across his body, a long, lingering cut through the air, the blade rising and lowering, following the contours of his body. She held his organ now in her left hand, the blade in her right. He heard himself, his voice shrill, tight, shouting, "No!"

She stopped, suddenly, letting go of him, the sword held high in both her hands.

There was a sound like the rush of air and the circle opened again, this time to his left, and suddenly the darkness beyond the circle was no longer darkness—but a ring of torches, torches more numerous than those surrounding him. The ring—the second ring to his left—opened. And beyond it was what appeared to be an altar. It was at the height of what looked almost like a stage, red-carpeted steps leading up to it. Unconsciously, he counted the steps—there were seven. He remembered something Bess had said about what they called the "majik" number—seven. It stood for chaos, Bess had— "Bess!" Frost heard himself shout the word before he realized he had said it.

A woman, arms outstretched at her sides, her body painted with symbols on the abdomen, on the face, her eyes wide, her mouth open as if screaming but no sound coming from it, naked. She was being dragged, herded across the stage toward the altar, a man on either side of her, holding her arms and wrists, the men black robed. And suddenly, finally, she screamed, "Frost!"

The one-eyed man felt the tendons in his neck distending, the muscles in his arms and legs going taut, the pain in his head vibrating his entire body now.

At the rear of the altar, as Bess, screaming Frost's name over and over again, was dragged upon it, stood a figure, robed, but robed differently from the rest.

A hood concealed the face, and massive shoulders seemed to fill out the red satin folds of the robe. Strange designs were embroidered upon the robe. As the figure began to talk, the arms rose, the robe fell open; the body under it was naked—at least from the waist up where Frost could see. The robe seemed lined—ridiculously he thought—with white lace, like a tablecloth or the curtains in a country cottage.

And the voice—ti was one Frost recognized.

"Death, disembowelment. We shall cut the flesh, consume it, and drink the blood. We shall punish those who persecute us, defile the Damned One, the one who is our master!"

The naked woman with the bizarre body painting left the circle of hooded figures surrounding the slab on which Frost lay. Gravely, she ascended the steps, holding the bizarre short sword in both her hands. As she reached the height of the steps, the man from behind the altar walked around it, his hands tracing across Bess's breasts and abdomen. He stood before the naked and sweating painted woman.

The woman dropped to her knees, the sword hilt upraised and offered in her hands, but the blade pointed toward her, its tip against her left breast, over the heart.

The man—the priest?—reached to her and took the sword, never moving its tip.

Then suddenly he raised the sword, high above her, the blade aimed toward the darkness where the torchlight couldn't reach. The woman stooped, her face low to the red-carpeted floor before the altar, her lips touching the man's bare feet. He raised the skirt of the robe, exposing the naked lower half of his body. The woman moved her mouth up along the man's feet, then to his legs and knees and suddenly, clutching with both her hands, she kissed the man's buttocks.

At this, she fell back, thighs wide apart, on her knees, hands and arms outstretched, as if offering him her body.

The man raised his voice, shouting, "Satani!"

The voice— Frost felt the nausea sweeping him, making him choke. He tugged at the rope holding his right wrist.

The voice belonged to Dr. Lassiter Kulley.

Chapter Fifteen

Kulley returned to the rear of the altar. Bess was stretched out across it now, tied, screaming, screaming so long and so loudly her voice was hoarse, cracked. Frost had heard of people who had screamed so long with pain or terror that they had forever afterward lost the power of speech. He ripped at his flesh now, trying to tear his right hand free of the rope which bound it. He felt a searing pain, then a warm wetness. The rope still held him firm.

Kulley dipped the blade of the short sword into a silver container. Its shape was similar to that of a bucket, but it was set on a short pedestal, somewhat like a chalice.

"The blood of the ram to make more acceptable the sacrifice!" Kulley's voice echoed, boomed over the chanting as he dipped the blade in and out, the blade now dripping red blood.

"No!" Frost shouted as Kulley laid the blade across Bess's naked abdomen. Kulley started to move the blade, using it to paint her flesh with the blood of the dead animal—one sacrificial victim coloring another.

Bess screamed, "Frost!"

Dancing now, their robes gone, the Satanists held their torches high with their left hands, the flames catching the sweating flesh of their naked bodies and the gleaming steel of blades in their light.

As the blade of the woman with the painted body

140

had done, the knives sliced through the air above him, sometimes resting momentarily against his flesh, then arcing up, high and away, only to slice down near him again, perilously close.

Bess screamed, Kulley intoned the power of Satan, the dancers chanted and shrieked, each of them in turn dancing past the altar, past the chalice, dipping their blades in it, slicing their blades wildly through the air over Bess as she writhed there on the stone altar, her abdomen, her breasts, her face now painted red with the blood of the ram.

Frost, tugging at the rope on his right wrists, suddenly felt it crushing against the fleshy part of his hand beneath his thumb joint. He could feel the skin ripping. Sweat from the dancers sprayed over him; blood dripped on him from their knives.

The one-eyed man pulled against his right hand, with all the strength he had. Pain in his wrist. The rawness, the cutting of the rope against raw flesh. The ache in his head and neck. The nausea that had never stopped.

"Free!"

He shouted it, but no one heard him.

As one of the dancers—a woman—sliced her blade through the air above his face, the one-eyed man reached up, blood dripping down his forearm from his torn wrist. His right hand grasped the hand of the woman, the knife clutched in it. He tore the hand, smashing it down against the stone slab on which he lay. The woman's fingers opened; the woman screamed, but her scream was lost in the tumult of voices around them.

Frost's right fist gripped the killing knife, and he slashed, across the front of the woman's throat, the tip of the blade hooking into her left nostril as he ripped it upward, partially cutting her nose away. Blood

141

sprayed across his chest and face as he moved the knife.

He chopped at the rope on his left wrist; the rope frayed, his skin bled from the knife. He pulled; the rope snapped. He hacked apart the rope across his abdomen.

Knives were slicing at him as he leaned forward—nausea, pain, all of it drowning him. He hacked free his right ankle; blood spurted from his skin as the knife blade cut too deep. A sword was chopping down toward him. Frost reached into the crowd of devil-worshipers, snatching at a man by his shoulder-length hair, throwing the body across his own, like a shield.

The sword drove home; the man screamed, his body shuddering. Frost rolled the body away, hacked free his left ankle, then half-rolled, half-fell from the slab to the stone floor!

He felt knives cutting at him, heard the whooshing of swords somehow above the screams and the chanting. He rammed his knife blade forward, into the chest of a man starting to turn toward him, in the man's right hand a sword.

The body lurched back. Frost's right hand lost the knife, but snatched at the sword.

The one-eyed man's right fist balled around the ornately carved hilt and he shouted, "Die!" The sword flashed downward in his hand, cleaving the skull of the nearest devil-worshiper.

Suddenly, the chanting, the screaming—he realized it had all stopped.

He didn't know if it was the residual effect of the drug, or an adrenaline level higher than he had ever known, or perhaps a combination of the two mingled with the terrible pain from where he had been struck in the head.

But, blood dripping down his forearm as he held the

142

sword high ahead of him, naked, angry, wanting to kill, the one-eyed man felt suddenly, inexplicably invincible.

The ring of devil-worshipers was a disordered route now, some few fighting their way through the mass of naked, sweating bodies, toward him, but the others fleeing. He thought that it might have seemed different to them—slaughtering a helpless woman or child, a victim—different from seeing themselves slaughtered.

A man raced toward him with a sword flashing in his hands, a scream on his lips.

Frost side-stepped and swung the blade through the air. The blade caught, the head of the swordsman toppling from his shoulders as his body fell away. The head rolled across the floor, the eyes wide open. A woman was screaming, men were running from it.

Frost started toward the altar. The crimson-robed Dr. Lassiter Kulley stood with the ceremonial killing sword poised over Bess's throat. "Drop the sword, Captain Frost—or your woman is dead!"

"You might make it out of here alive—if you're lucky and let her go," Frost answered, standing unsteadily now before the satanic altar, opposite Kulley. Bess, her eyes wide disks of terror, was between them, prostrate. "But if you touch her, you won't get more than a step. I swear that to God—not your god, but the real one." Frost held the sword, up near his right shoulder, the blade ready to cleave Kulley's head from the shoulders.

"You—"

"Drop the killing sword—then move back. Lay it across her abdomen—so I can use it to cut her free."

"No—you can't—"

"I know. You were only foolin'—just wanted to scare us. Well—I'm so scared that if you blink you're

143

dead."

"I—"

"Talk about it in your next sermonette. Now drop the damned sword!"

Frost never moved his own sword, keeping it poised, ready to snap out. Kulley bent slightly to set down the sword, then dropped suddenly behind the altar. Frost hacked for him, but missed. The one-eyed man heard the screams behind him, the shouts, the curses as he picked up the killing sword in his left hand. He sliced away the bonds on Bess's right wrist, then the left, then those on her ankles. And as he turned, a horde of the devil-worshipers were starting up the altar steps toward him. Bess sat up, her naked arms wrapped around his chest.

Frost hurled the killing sword toward the Satanists, then grabbed Bess by her right hand with his left, half-dragging her from the altar stone and onto the seven carpeted steps.

He loosed her hand, rasping, "Right behind me, kid." Then, holding the sword at shoulder height, he started toward the momentarily stalled crowd of satanic cultists. The knot of naked, knife- and sword-armed devil-worshipers opened, Frost and Bess passing into it, the opening then closing behind them.

"Frost, we're boxed in!"

"Boy! Are they in trouble," the one-eyed man half-whispered.

They were halfway across the floor now. The torches there which still burned and billowed oily black smoke cast a bizarre, almost blood-washed light over the entire chamber. At its farthest limit were double doors. Beside them, flanking the doors, were two men, still robed, and holding massive swords, larger than the rest, poised to strike.

"Doormen," Frost snapped. "Every organization

needs a sergeant at arms who's a good bouncer, I guess." He spoke as though he were going crazy and he realized that perhaps he was—or he was already there.

Her voice trembling, her hands on his naked back, Bess murmured, "Now's the time to tell me how you've gotten out of tighter spots than this one, Frost."

"Well," he answered, not looking at her, "there was the time in the harem; I got stuck using a sword there, fighting these eunuchs. They were built like brick shithouses—every one of them.* Then—"

The voice shouting, screaming from behind them, made his blood run colder than it already was. "Throw down your sword—or you both die!"

"Go to hell, Kulley—they got a reservation for ya!" Frost shouted back.

"Kill them! Now!"

The circle around them began to tighten, swords and knives outstretched toward them. "Twenty yards to the door—when I cut a hole in the people, run for it," Frost rasped. A sword swiped toward him; the one-eyed man parried it, side-stepping, hacking his blade in a broad arc, missing the original swordsman who'd made the lunge, cutting across the chest of another, hacking off part of the left arm of a third man.

He wheeled, slicing the sword into the crowd behind them, then dodged, narrowly missing Bess as she avoided his lunge. A knife-wielding woman screamed, threw herself toward him. Frost impaled the woman on the sword, losing it in her chest as he pushed her back into the crowd. There was a narrow opening in the throng just ahead of them, and Frost reached out, grabbing Bess's hand, racing toward the opening with

*See: They Call Me the Mercenary #7, *Slave of the Warmonger*.

145

her.

Knives slashed at him, opening cuts across his back; fists hammered at him. He smashed his right fist out, the inside of his right forearm cut now as he grazed the edge of a killing knife. His fist connected with the nose of a woman Satanist, hammering her back against the sword blade of a man behind her. She screamed.

Frost felt hands grabbing at his throat, his left elbow snapped back, meeting flesh and bone. A scream. Then the hands released him. He pushed Bess ahead of him now, almost knocking her from her feet, through the opening in the mass of satanic cultists. Frost grabbed her, started to run; the two men beside the door, their vastly more massive swords poised, waited for him.

The one-eyed man loosed Bess's hands. He snatched up a torch from the floor, swiping with it toward their pursuers, catching the hair of one of the men on fire, the arm of one of the women. There was screaming. A sword crashed down toward him. Frost blocked it with the torch; the torch cleaved in two. Frost's left knee snapped up into the naked crotch of the man with the sword, doubling him over.

Frost hammered his balled-together fists down across the back of the man's neck, breaking it, grabbing the sword in his right hand.

He lunged with it, its point penetrating the Adam's apple of a knife-wielder coming toward him.

"Frost!"

It was Bess and as he parried another knife blade, then cleaved off the hand holding it, he wheeled. The robed guards were coming at him from the doors.

Frost pushed Bess aside, and reaching down, snatched up a torch.

The sword in his right hand, the torch in his left, he edged away from the crowd which now held back,

146

letting the door guards do their work. The swords they held were at least a foot longer than the one Frost held in his hand, and at least two inches wider—thicker, too, it seemed. Each man held his sword in both hands, like a broad sword.

The nearer of the two, the one to Frost's left, struck out with his sword; Frost dodged right. The second swordsman was coming for him now. Frost dropped to his knees, then rolled, the torch in his left hand swinging out, catching the hem of the black robe of the swordsman. The robe was suddenly aflame, the swordsman screaming.

Frost climbed to his feet. The first swordsman stepped back; the second man—like a torch now, the entire skirt of his robe in flames that licked upward and caught at the base of his hood—threw himself toward the one-eyed man.

When Frost parried the blade, his own sword was cut in two. The sheet of flame that had been human dropped to the stone floor, a hideous scream echoing across the hall.

Frost picked up the dead guard's massive sword, as the first man charged at him. Frost dropped to one knee, bracing the sword against the stone floor. The swordsman saw it too late, his abdomen punched against it, and the blade impaled him.

Bess shouted. "Frost—I've got the doors!"

The one-eyed man was on his feet, weaponless now, edging back, the crowd storming toward him. He picked up one torch, then a second, flashing them like some kind of Tahitian dancer so that the torches burned the skin, the hair of the people pressing toward him. He hurled the first torch into the crowd, then the second.

He felt something against his foot, then looked down—the sword of the second door guard had slid

147

across the floor. Frost bent and picked it up. "A Magnum—wow!" he gasped.

A swordsman from the knot of pursuers came at him in a run; Frost chopped through his blade and split his chest at the breast bone; the body reeled back, spurting blood.

He felt Bess's hand at his elbow. "Frost—the doors!"

The one-eyed man glanced behind him a second—daylight through broad picture windows—an open hallway. He grabbed Bess's right hand in his left and started to run, the screams of the burned and wounded satanic blood cultists filling the air from behind him.

The hallway was long, almost barren of furniture save for leather-covered benches spaced approximately every twenty feet. He ran the hallway's length, Bess beside him now, with perhaps a dozen of the Satanists—still naked and armed with blades—in close pursuit.

"Frost! Look out there!" Still running, Frost glanced to his left. Bess was pointing beyond one of the picture windows toward an almost idyllic-looking white-fenced horse pasture.

"So?" he gasped, breathless.

"The horses—we can ride out of here."

"You know how to ride. I don't!"

"Frost! They'll catch us otherwise!"

"Nuts," he rasped, feeling good, feeling strong—realizing the drug and the adrenaline flow were making him high. He skidded to a halt on his bare feet. Armed guards were coming toward them from the other end of the hall—these armed with assault rifles rather than swords. "Just made up my mind," he shouted to Bess.

He dropped the sword to the tiled floor beneath his feet and picked up one of the leather-upholstered

148

benches. He had it up, over his head, when he called to Bess, "Look away!" He hurled the bench toward the picture window. The glass shattered, an alarm instantly sounding, a screeching klaxon that for an instant at least drowned out the curses of the Satanists less than a dozen yards behind them.

Frost picked up the sword, smashing away the shards of glass as he approached the window, clearing the bottom of the window frame. "Watch the glass!" he ordered, going through ahead of her, helping her side-step a jagged shard half-buried in the muddy dirt near his feet. Beside him now, she started to run. Frost looked back once. The Satanists were holding back, the men with the assault rifles almost parallel to the broken window.

Frost bent into a dead run, the sword rowing the air at his side as he ran after Bess toward the horse pasture.

She was clambering over the fence by the time he reached it. Already the bursts of automatic-weapon fire were starting; the ground near his feet was churning under the impact of the assault-rifle slugs.

Frost climbed up the fence, dropping over it; Bess already approached the nearest of the horses. The animal back-stepped. Bess almost cooing to it as she reached out, grabbing the mane. "Here—Frost—this one!"

Shaking his head, then glancing back and seeing the assault rifle–armed guards streaking across the ground after them, he ran toward the horse. It was brown; from somewhere he remembered you called it a bay. "Girl horse or boy horse?" he asked.

"A mare—"

"I wasn't asking about its politics."

"A girl—get on!"

Frost looked at the animal, then reached up. There

149

wasn't any saddle. "I don't know how!"

"Gimme the sword!" she ordered him. She took it, then said, "Hold the mane—the long hair up front on the neck—with your left hand, the rump—the butt—with your right, and then swing up."

"Ohh." Frost did as she told him, suddenly finging himself on the back of the horse; the animal moved under his bare skin. "Ha! The hair tickles!"

"Shut up!" she screamed, handing him the sword, then running toward another of the animals.

The armed guards were less than twenty yards back now, some of them dropping to kneeling positions, firing. A bullet tore at Frost's left shoulder; blood spurted from the fresh wound. His horse reared up on its hind legs and the one-eyed man held onto the mane with both fists, the sword pinned under his arm.

"That's the way to do it!" Bess screamed encouragingly. He looked around. She was swinging aboard a white horse with black mane and stockings.

"Come on—use your knees," she called, starting her own animal into a gallop across the pasture.

"Aww—I don't—" Frost rasped, then nudged the horse with his knees. The horse leaped ahead, after Bess and the white horse she rode.

Frost held his mount's mane with both hands, his knuckles white. There was more gunfire behind them now and Frost glanced back, his breath coming in short gasps. He was terrified, not of the gunmen as he should have been, not of the fight with the Satanists—but riding a horse, especially bareback, scared him to death.

The alarm that had sounded inside the building was now sounding across the grounds as well and as Frost clung to the animal beneath him, he heard still another sound, above that of the alarm, above the sporadic gunfire and shouting, it was the yelping of dogs.

Holding on more tightly, he glanced behind him—Dobermans, a half-dozen at least, racing after them.

He remembered the word from the cowboy movies. He shouted to the horse, "Gyaagh!" It evidently meant something to horses, the one-eyed man decided, because the animal leaped ahead and ran.

Chapter Sixteen

"How do you stop a horse?" the one-eyed man called out.

"Pull back on the mane and shout whoa!"

Frost tugged at the flowing brown hair of the animal he rode, pulling back, calling out, "Whoa! Come on and stop horse!" The animal slowed; Frost slid forward but stayed aboard.

The dog pack was two hundred yards behind them, closing fast now that they had stopped their frantic ride. Motorized pursuers came as well—business suit-clad security men carrying M-16s riding in pickup trucks and open-top four-wheel-drive jeeps. The Satanists who had pursued them from the vast hall where the slaughter had been scheduled to take place were nowhere in evidence. Ahead of Frost, his horse rearing under him, scaring him, was a vast fence, its height twelve feet, barbed wire across its top. The construction of the fence—barbed wire laced through the chain link—did not lend itself to scaling.

"What'll we do, Frost?"

"Ride," the one-eyed man snapped. "Along the fence line—gotta be a gate!" His head screamed at him with every bump and jar from the animal under him; his arms, his chest, his back were a mass of small cuts and deeper, bleeding lacerations. He still had the sweet taste of the drugged coffee in his mouth, and he realized he was behaving bizarrely.

"Ride!" The one-eyed man kneed the animal under him; the animal lurched ahead, sweat from its neck and chest spraying him, his hair ripped by the wind. "I'm insane," he murmured into the wind. He was enjoying himself; the chase, the danger, even now riding the horse. He loosed the mane with his right hand, snatching at the massive sword under his left arm, wielding it in his right as two assault rifle–armed guards raced at them from out of a hedgerow.

Frost kneed the animal harder, racing down on them, the sword high in his right hand, a shout on his lips, his throat aching with it. "Die!" The nearer of the two men fired his assault rifle. Frost's animal reared under him as Frost swiped down with the massive sword, lopping off the left arm of his attacker. Frost hacked with the sword again as the body began to fall, his blade cleaving the head from the shoulders.

The second man stood there, paralyzed, the assault rifle poised to fire in his hands, but silent.

Frost's horse came down. The one-eyed man, naked, bleeding, thinking himself insane, kneed the animal gently forward, confident now that he could ride it.

The guard slowly made to raise his rifle. Frost hauled back the sword to his right shoulder, the blade ready to swing out.

"Wait—please," the man murmured, then dropped the gun to his side.

Frost studied the man's face, feeling the pace of his heart subsiding, his breathing becoming regular again. He lowered the sword slightly, not wanting to kill. The security man suddenly brought up the rifle, firing a wild burst. Frost's horse reared. Frost cleaved the sword outward as the animal died under him. The sword beheaded the assault rifle–armed guard, and Frost's own body tumbled across his.

153

The one-eyed man pushed himself back from the headless corpse. "My God," he whispered. Somehow, he thought of the word "barbarism," murmuring it to himself.

"Frost?"

The one-eyed man looked up. Bess was still astride her horse, its black mane a sharp contrast against the white of the animal's body and the flesh of her own.

"I'm all right now," he almost whispered.

The one-eyed man dropped the sword and picked up the assault rifle. He wondered then, in a brief flash of logic or perhaps something else, what the difference was between the bloodied sword and this? He began, methodically, to strip the pants from the dead man. He pulled them on. Forcing his feet into the shoes, he realized they were too small and kicked them away. The shirt had only a few bloodstains on it, so Frost took it from the body, then handed it up to Bess to use. She looked at it a moment, at the bloodstains, then put it on. The animal blood that Kulley had painted on her body mingled with the beads of sweat that dripped from her breasts and abdomen and face.

"Frost—is this real?"

He couldn't answer, simply nodding his head. Under the man's coat, there had been a bloodied shoulder holster, a revolver in it. In the jacket pockets were loose cartridges and speedloaders. Frost put these inside the pockets of the borrowed pants.

He searched the first body, quickly, finding more ammo for the assault rifles, but not another handgun. He pulled the pants from the dead man, then looked up at Bess. "Here—put these on."

"There isn't—the dogs—the—"

"There's time," he told her calmly. "Here. Use it on yourself if you have to. I love you." He handed her the revolver. He moved around the dead horse he had ridden, kissing Bess's mouth once, quickly, as he stood beside her.

One assault rifle across his back, a second in his right hand, he stooped to pick up the sword. He wiped the blood from it on the grass near his bare feet, then slipped the sword through the belt holding up his borrowed pants. The belt held it in place.

Now less than a hundred yards from them he could see, first the dog pack, then the armed men. There was no escape other than to fight and die or be victorious. It was the story of his life.

Chapter Seventeen

"Get on your horse and ride—away from here. The gates should be up ahead. They won't expect you there, with me here and the gunfire. You'll have a chance if there's only one guard, or two. I taught you how to use one of these." He gestured toward the Smith & Wesson revolver in her right hand. She looked ridiculous, the bloodstained man's shirt, the borrowed, vastly too large trousers, the look of terror in her eyes, her blond hair wind-tossed and streaming sweat.

"No—with you or not at all."

"Let the horse go then—get it out of here. But save a bullet for yourself. It's better than . . ." He just shook his head, feeling her hand squeeze his.

As she released the horse, swatting its rump hard and shouting, Frost started running toward the trees beyond the hedgerow and the body of the dead horse. He called to her. "Come on!"

The farthest vehicle was twenty-five yards away; all the vehicles stopped. The dog pack was closing in.

Using a tree for cover, Bess behind him now, Frost raised the assault rifle to his shoulder, the selector on semi. He would need full-auto for the men who would follow the dogs.

He triggered the first shot. The lead Doberman winced, tumbled through the air, falling; the other dogs sniffed at him for a moment, then raced on as

Frost fired again. Another animal down. He cursed the men who had trained them to kill, wishing instead he were killing them, firing again and again, more of the animals going down. One of the dogs made it through. Frost rammed it in the teeth as it lunged for them, cracking the butt of the M-16 against the skull of the animal. He shouldered the rifle again, firing. The magazine was empty, and five of the dogs were still coming. No time for a fresh stick, or the second rifle across his back, Frost dropped the first rifle, pushing Bess behind him. The dogs lunged, and the massive sword came into his hands. He cleaved the air with it, beheading one of the Dobermans, slicing across the chest of another.

He hacked back with the sword, gutting a third attack dog; a fourth and fifth dog lunged for him.

"Frost!"

The fourth dog knocked Frost back, hammering him to the ground, its jaws wide at his throat. The sword gone, Frost's fingers closed on the animal's throat. He heard a gunshot, felt the dog's body shudder over him, then slump. There was a second shot; the fifth dog rolled to the ground, then sprang up, coming for Bess as Frost got to his knees. He picked up the sword, screaming as he heaved it, chopping the animal down as it lunged for Bess's face.

Frost climbed to his feet, unslinging the second assault rifle. "Load that other one," Frost commanded. "The men will be coming." Already the nearest of the jeeps was starting across the grassy expanse beyond the trees, the hedgerow, and the body of the dead horse.

There were ten men, at least, assault rifles already blazing from the rear ends of the pickup trucks.

Frost opened fire; Bess knelt beside him in the trees, the other assault rifle to her shoulder, bullets ripping into the tree trunks around them. Bess screamed once, and Frost looked to her, saw the left sleeve of the borrowed and already bloodied shirt bloodier still and wet. She kept firing; Frost fired, a bullet tearing across the top of his left shoulder, shoving him back. He forced the pain from his mind, still firing.

A long burst of concentrated automatic-weapon fire hammered into the trees. Frost's legs went out from under him, and as he fell, he could see some of the men clambering out of the jeeps, pushing the bodies of the dead ahead of them. He reshouldered his rifle, firing still. The gun was empty; at least four of the men were still alive, coming. Bess dropped one, her rifle empty now as well.

"The pistol!" Frost snatched it from her, killing the third man. Only two remained.

A burst of automatic-weapon fire cut into him as Bess picked up the revolver, firing it twice; the head of the second man exploded as he fell back.

Bess, limping, her left arm hanging bloodied at her side, stumbled back, shielding Frost where he fell, her body against his. "Go ahead—damn you!" she screamed.

The fourth man raised his assault rifle, then pulled the trigger. Nothing happened.

"Goddamn you," he muttered, then started reaching under his coat as the rifle dropped from his hands.

Frost lurched his body forward, Bess toppling back from him. His right hand found the sword and he raised it, ramming it up and forward, into the gunman's testicles. There was a scream, and the automatic pistol the man drew from under his coat discharged into the air. His body fell.

Frost bled heavily from his left side, from his left thigh and his right calf. Bess's left arm was useless; her face was pale, drained by pain and loss of blood,

158

but her right fist locked onto the steering wheel of the pickup truck they'd stolen.

Ahead of them were the gates. Sirens no longer wailed behind them; no more guards or dogs pursued them. Two guards, without rifles, but each holding a handgun stood at the double chain-link gate.

"Last ones, kid," Frost murmured, barely able to sit up. The .45 Colt automatic was in his right fist, with seven rounds left after the one fired from the hand of the man he'd disemboweled. There had been no spare magazines. Frost raised the gun as Bess hammered down on the accelerator, toward the gates. He fired through the passenger-side open window; the two guards were already firing at them. The windshield cracked but didn't shatter. Bess cut the wheel hard right, straight at the gates.

Frost fired again, then again, nailing the one to his right; the man's body crumpled. Frost fired across the hood, leaning half from the cab of the pickup, four shots, the last two connecting, spinning the body of the remaining guard into the path of the truck. Frost felt the lurch and bump as Bess drove over the man, then the shudder as the pickup crashed through the gates.

"No hospital, kid—O'Hara first," he rasped, closing his eye, trying to stay conscious.

Chapter Eighteen

She hadn't liked his little apartment in South Bend, but then he hadn't really liked it either. She'd told him the picture he'd kept of her with the face cut out—the face picture he carried in his wallet—had been strange, but right after that she'd told him that she loved him for it. He had closed down the apartment, packing his folding chair, his TV table and his 1969–vintage black-and-white portable that he'd bought for the first lunar landing, and stuffing all of it into the trunk of the first car he had actually owned in more than five years. He had always used a Diablo Protective Services car. They had visited Bess's parents living outside Chicago, explaining as little as possible about why he limped and why under the long sleeves of her blouses or dresses Bess's left arm was bandaged and why she moved it stiffly.

Six weeks in the hospital had righted the wound in his left side, but he still took it easy when he could; the muscle there was not completely healed yet. Bess had explained to her parents as Frost had loaded her suitcases into the car—"Yes, I love him. We're not getting married yet. We're going to live together—in a suburb of Atlanta. You haven't heard of it. I'll write as soon as we settle in." Then, "He made a lot of money once. We can live on that and what I make; my bureau's transferring me back from London. He'll find something to do. He loves me. It'll be all right." Then, "He always carries a gun. It's just something he does, that's all."

After that, they had driven away, the gently used 1978 LTD he had bought humming them along the highway. He had bought it because he liked full-sized cars and they didn't make full-sized cars anymore, he had explained to Bess. She had smiled, telling him they didn't make Hank Frosts anymore either.

It was a large apartment they rented, just north of Atlanta proper. The weather was beautiful, the days long and the nights short. The one-eyed man and the woman who had fought beside him, nearly died beside him, and had loved him since they'd first met, at last came to know one another.

After three weeks of getting "settled in," Bess's arm completely healed. Frost was able to run three miles each morning and the leg wound no longer made him limp. Then there was a call on their newly installed telephone.

Bess had caught it just as they had been coming inside, late on a Thursday night, ideas of starships and aliens fresh in their heads from the movie they had seen.

"It's for you," she said, her smile curious.

Frost took the telephone. "Yeah?"

"Well, if it isn't the old retired mercenary with the rotten sense of humor."

"Mike. How are ya?"

"Thought maybe you and Bess might invite me over for dinner—and I could tell you about it. What'dya say, huh?"

"When are you in town?"

"Will be tomorrow. Got a little business early in the day. Maybe I could come over after that, chew the fat, eat some of Bess's cooking. Can't let you be livin' with a dame that don't know how ta cook—give her the old

O'Hara taste test."

"Wonderful." Frost smiled into the receiver, really meaning the word for a change. "Six or so—unless you can get over earlier. Earlier's better—longer to talk that way."

"Good. And unless you move you can't avoid me—I got your address already."

"Just shut up and come on over, Mike." Frost laughed.

"Hey. Give her my love huh? But just the friend kind."

Frost nodded into the receiver, realizing O'Hara couldn't see him, then added, "Yeah, sure I will, Mike. Be good to see you."

The line clicked off, and Frost studied the receiver a moment, then set it down.

"He's coming for dinner?" Bess asked, setting down her purse beside the telephone.

"Sent you his love—just the friend kind, he said."

"That's good—'cause I don't need any more of the other kind." She came into the one-eyed man's arms. . . .

They made love for a very long time that night, Bess doing the things to him that drove him crazy yet pleased him, Frost laboring lovingly over her body to prolong her pleasure, to make her feel what she wanted to feel. Then afterward the two of them settled into each other's arms.

"Did he say what he was coming to town for?" Bess asked after a while.

"Mike? No. Probably some more of his top-secret crap."

"Why did we move back here? I mean after—"

Frost laughed. "Maybe we killed all the serious bad guys in and around Atlanta when we busted out of that place. I don't know."

162

"We didn't think it was finished, did we?"

"I guess not," he told her. "Kulley never even got arrested, had an iron-clad alibi for the whole night that they had us. When O'Hara got out to that estate, there weren't any bodies, just a lot of bullet holes and bloodstains. No evidence."

"I'll bet it's another one of those missing scientists," she whispered, her lips close to his ear.

"Maybe—like the ones O'Hara was talking about?"

"Yeah. I saw something in this morning's paper about another one of them turning up missing."

"Could be that. I don't think even O'Hara would try nailing Lassiter Kulley again."

"You know," she murmured, "the other day when you were out at the pistol range? I turned on the TV. I saw Kulley giving another one of his sermons, talking about devil-worshipers, witches, condemning them. What a damned hypocrite!"

"Yeah. Maybe I should do like I said."

"No. If you kill him, you'll be the one the law will go after. This is the first time in either one of our lives we've been happy. Let's not ruin—"

Frost leaned over her, pulling her up to him, crushing her mouth under his; her arms went around his neck, her fingers kneading his flesh. "Ouch!" He laughed.

After a while, she fell asleep, as she usually did, her head resting against his chest. He stared up at the ceiling. It was the first time in weeks he had thought about Kulley, about the coverup of the dead men at the estate, the estate itself—owned by a blind corporation. He wondered what had happened to Martin. He knew it was Martin who had come into Kulley's office; Martin the killer, the murderer, the one with friends high up enough to whitewash whatever he did, to give him anonymity.

He eased Bess's head down onto the pillow, then sat in the darkness. After a time, he reached across to the night stand, taking the battered Zippo, flicking back the cowling, and rolling the striking wheel under his thumb to light a Camel. He inhaled the smoke hard. As he started to put down the Zippo, he relit the lighter; the light from the blue-yellow flame illuminated enough of the darkness on the night stand for him to see what he had wanted to see. The thought of Kulley and Martin, still out there, had made seeing it an imperative—the Metalife SS Chromium M–finished Browning High Power.

He balled his left fist tight in the darkness. Something made him think he'd be using it soon again, and not just for paper targets.

Chapter Nineteen

Six o'clock had come, then seven, then seven-forty-five. O'Hara had not come. By eight-thirty, Bess had rewarmed the beef stroganoff and made fresh noodles and the two of them sat alone, eating, silent.

By nine-forty-five, Bess said, "Go ahead. Call FBI headquarters. See what happened to Mike."

"You think I should? You know O'Hara. He might have been down here on his own, never told them about it."

"Go ahead."

Frost got to his feet, holding Bess's chair for her as she got up; and as she started into the kitchen with two hands full of dishes, Frost sat down beside the telephone. He started to dial directory assistance, then heard a buzzer—the doorbell being rung from the downstairs hallway.

He stood up, saying, "Must be Mike—can you warm it up again?"

"I'll fix something he'll like. Don't worry," she called back, her voice almost drowned by the sound of running water from the kitchen sink.

He pushed the door buzzer to release the downstairs door lock so O'Hara could enter the main lobby. He heard the water stop, then Bess saying, "Frost, what if that wasn't O'Hara?"

Frost's fists balled tight, and he started across the room, breaking into a run, reaching the bedroom, throwing open the closet door, and reaching inside his suitbag where he had the Interdynamics KG-99 hung on its sling. He shook the sling loose, working open the bolt, letting it slam forward, chambering the top round from the thirty-six-round stick. He depressed the cocking knob, the safety, then started back toward the door. "Stay in the kitchen—just in case."

"What? What if it's somebody selling magazines?"

Frost looked at the semiautomatic in his hands. It resembled a submachine gun. He shrugged. "I won't buy any. I don't like subscribing to things."

There was a knock on the apartment door. Frost approached it, but stood to the side.

The knock came again, gently. Frost called out, "Who is it?"

"It's Roger Cummins, Captain Frost, Special Agent in Charge, Federal Bureau of Investigation."

"Who's with you?"

"You don't know him—but he's a government employee as well. May we come in?"

Frost held the KG-99 in his right hand, opening the door with his left, stepping back.

He saw Cummins and the other man eye the gun. Frost smiled. "This thing—just getting ready to clean it. Come on. Buy you a cup of coffee."

"Thank you." Cummins nodded, stepping inside, the other man, tall, thin, white-haired, following after him. "This is Ray Costigan—he's ahh, with—"

"CIA, Captain Frost. You should recognize one of these." The white-haired man produced a small vinyl-window wallet. Frost recognized the seal, the signature.

Frost handed back the identity case, then took Costigan's outstretched hand. "Mr. Costigan—contract or—"

"I signed up for the duration—a long time ago."

166

Costigan smiled, running the fingers of his left hand through his white hair. "That coffee sounds good."

Frost looked across the great room at Bess standing behind the kitchen counter. "You wanna give these guys some coffee, kid?"

She smiled, shrugging her shoulders. "Sure. Why not. Save a phone call, I guess."

"Phone call?" Cummins asked.

"What happened to Mike O'Hara?"

"Ohh." Cummins nodded. "Funny thing—I came here to ask you pretty much the same question."

From the kitchen, Frost heard Bess drop a coffee cup or plate. . . .

Bess didn't look at Frost when she brought the coffee. Frost watched her. She seemed to be studying her dark blue skirt as she smoothed it over her crossed legs. Finally, she looked up, saying not to Frost but to Costigan, "We're listening, Mr. Costigan—but remember, I'm a reporter."

"And a very good one from what I understand." Costigan smiled. He sipped his coffee, then set the cup down.

"Would you like more coffee? I can listen from the kitchen."

"Yes, thank you," Costigan told her, a little bitingly, Frost thought.

Leaning back from the small dinette table, Frost lit a cigarette and said, "What the hell is going on?"

"You are the only man who knows Vassily Vocienkov—by sight, not just a drawing."

"Who is—? Naw. Let me guess." The one-eyed man smiled. "Martin?"

Costigan smiled. "Yes, your Mr. Martin."

"What's Martin got to do with Mike O'Hara?"

"Well, not necessarily anything, but probably he killed O'Hara or—"

167

"Or what!" Frost suddenly realized he was no longer sitting, but standing, half-leaning across the small table, his right hand outstretched, inches from Costigan.

"Well, the more likely thing is that if they took him alive, well . . . they'd likely keep him alive—if you know what I mean. I mean— Well, O'Hara has been working against terrorists for a long time, involved in some pretty heavy stuff. Probably the KGB would want to sweat some things out of him—easier there than here."

"What do you mean easier there than here?" Frost asked, sitting down again, finding his cigarette. Bess was standing beside him, her hands pressed against her thighs. "Here." He gave her a cigarette.

She bent over while he lit it. "You mean Mike has been—"

"Probably, Miss Stallman." Cummins smiled.

"Why don't you start at point *A* and—"

"All right, Captain Frost." Costigan smiled again. "Back in Vietnam—your commanding officer. He was involved in tracking down a leak in U.S. intelligence. Kind of a peculiar leak. It wasn't strategic information going to the 'Cong, but strategic information going straight up the pipe into KGB headquarters, giving them the jump on American operations, American victories and defeats, letting their propaganda mill have it before our own newspapers had it—sometimes things our newspapers never got. It was very damaging, and gave the KGB an edge on our operations that we're still recovering from. Anyway, your old C.O. found his way into the pipeline and it's because of him we were able to choke it off. But because of that, Vocienkov killed him. We weren't able to go after Vocienkov because it would have blown what we knew about the KGB pipeline. So, he got away."

"Why didn't you go after him now?" Frost asked, realizing his voice was surprisingly calm.

"Similar reason, different operation—if anything, more serious than the last one. You . . ." Costigan said, sipping at the fresh coffee Bess poured for him, "you see, for some time we've been tape-recording the sermons of Dr. Lassiter Kulley."

"Ohh, shit," Frost murmured, shaking his head. "And you let us go through all that—nearly get butchered, that whole—holy—" Frost stood up, leaving the table and walking across the room toward the drape-covered windows leading to the small balcony. He pushed the drapes aside. As he smelled the fresh night air through the screen, he felt Bess beside him, her hands holding his left hand.

He turned around, facing Costigan; then, feeling himself trembling, his voice unsteady, said to Costigan, "You son of a bitch. You and everyone in your damned—"

"It was national security—in both instances. There are individual sacrifices that have to be—"

Frost ripped the eye patch from his face. "Individual sacrifices! Lose an eye, walk around all your life makin' up sick goddamned jokes over it! Tell me all about the little sacrifices we have to make!"

Bess was looking at him, strangely. "You mean—"

"Vietnam. A damned intelligence mission that was so hush-hush nobody could come and bail me out even though I was right smack in the middle of Saigon, three blocks from a headquarters building. And guys like you were sitting outside until they were through with me, could probably hear me scream when that bastard took a hot poker and—"

"No!" Bess threw her arms around him, crying. "Frost—my—"

Frost held her close against him, realizing, his skin

169

shivering from it, that for the first time since it had happened, he'd finally said why. He had never even verbalized it to himself.

"It was your job. You knew what the V.C. would do to you if they—"

"I used to think it would have been better if they'd killed me—you know that? And if Mike O'Hara's alive, what do you think they're gonna do to him—to make him talk? Who do you think the fuckin' V.C. learned it from? The KGB and the people they'd taught. Where's O'Hara?" Frost reached down to the couch, picking up the KG-99, then pulled out the bolt handle, the safety off. Cummins was reaching under his coat. Frost rasped, "I'll kill you—don't."

"Captain Frost, the reason we came," Costigan told him, "the reason we came was to admit we'd made a slight error—to ask for your help. I realize you're a mercenary and—"

"He's my friend!" Frost shouted.

"We wanted to offer you—"

"All right," Frost snapped, his throat tight with anger, the tendons of his neck distending against the collar of his shirt. "A million bucks—no reporting it to the government—tax free. And not to get O'Hara. I'll do that for free. But for you two bastards to get out of this room alive!"

Costigan smiled again. "I was authorized to go higher, actually. Deal."

Frost put down the KG-99, safing it. Kulley, Martin—they would tell him all of it now. He lit a cigarette, then very quietly said, "And if I don't make it, she gets it, or spills everything to the papers, the TV networks—the whole shot, so much that you couldn't even touch her for it."

Costigan nodded. Bess cried.

Chapter Twenty

The camouflage make-up itched his face and fingertips. He smiled, thinking that perhaps it would be the last time he'd ever use it. He had opted for his own weapons, rather than anything exotic Costigan and his CIA people could have provided. The KG-99 was strapped safely cross-body on its sling, in front of him now on his lap as he sat in the back seat of the 1979–vintage Lincoln Continental. The Metalifed Browning High Power was in the Cobra Gunskin rig under his left arm; spare magazines were stuffed in his pockets and in the off-gunside magazine pouch under his right arm. The little Gerber Mk-I boot knife was holstered at the small of his back.

He flexed his hands in the fingerless gloves. "I'm ready," he told Costigan.

"A radio . . . we could give you—"

"No. When you hear shots, come in. Otherwise drive away real fast. Because if I need your help and you fink out on me, well—you'd better hope I die, or I'll come and kill you."

"Agreed." Costigan nodded, clearing his throat.

Costigan got out so Frost could push the seat forward and climb out. He stood there, on the Georgia country road under the brilliant moonlight. He said to Costigan, "Funny—that dark of the moon thing—it's never the dark of the moon when you need it."

"Good luck," Costigan said, not extending his

hand.

Frost nodded, saying, "And remember something. Bess has sent copies of everything you told me by now, copies to friends in the publishing business, even one copy to a senator in Washington who's a friend of her father's. If I make it through and anything happens to either of us, or if I don't make it through and anything happens to her, well . . . You'll be spilled all over the newspapers and the wire services—"

"All right. I know that," Costigan snapped, angrily.

"You know, when I lost my eye, and they medically discharged me? Well, we'll consider this a pension—delayed." Frost turned and ran toward the tree line, a small knapsack on his left shoulder, with grenades, a gas mask, and other potentially useful items inside it.

He ran through the trees and toward the vine-covered stone fence, perhaps fifteen feet high. It was deceptive. Costigan had warned him that a thin set of wires ran across the top five feet of the fence, generating twenty-five thousand volts when touched.

Beyond it were silent alarm systems, armed men.

Frost mentally and physically shrugged. He studied the fence, then reached into the knapsack. The device looked like a pistol-gripped, sawed-off shotgun, but instead of an antipersonnel weapon, it fired a rappelling device, a three-pronged hook. The thought amused him; he wondered just how effective an antipersonnel device it might be.

Checking from side to side, ascertaining that no one he could see was watching him, the one-eyed man raced toward the fence, dropped to one knee, then braced the tiny butt of the rappelling device against the ground. He triggered it, the gun rocking in his hands. The three-pronged projectile arced upward, toward the top of the fence, disappearing over it.

172

Frost pulled the coil of rope toward him, making it taut, hearing a faint scraping sound against the top of the wall.

He reached into the canvas knapsack, taking the specially insulated boots and pulling them over his combat boots, as extra protection against the electrical current in the top five feet of the wall.

Discarding the shotgun-shaped launcher into the trees, ramming his fingers into insulated gloves, the one-eyed man ran for the wall, his hands knotted on the rope. He started up, the KG-99 dangling down his back now. His mouth and cheeks perspired under the black bandanna tied bandit fashion across the lower portion of his face, identical to the one tied over his hair.

He was at the last five-foot section of the wall now, seeing sparks crackling from the three-pronged hook on the top of the wall as he crossed over onto it, still careful not to touch the wall surface with his gloved hands; the core of the rope was grounded to bleed current down into the ground as he climbed.

He kicked the three-pronged hook with his foot, guiding it with the rope, loosing it to a crackle of sparks, then re-hooking it, but with the prongs facing opposite so he could rappel down the wall now, onto the grounds of the Kulley estate.

He let down the length of rope, the hook secured, then started down, his hands almost brushing the wall as he did. He murmured to himself, "Glad you wore the rubber gloves, Frost."

He was past the five-foot electrified section, pausing now to scan the interior of the grounds again. He saw nothing, except lights from the big house beyond the trees. The absence of security worried him more than a possible lurking presence.

"O'Hara," he rasped under his breath.

He started the rest of the way down the wall, dropping the last few feet, then snapping the line, the hook freeing and tumbling to the ground beside him. Frost recoiled the rope, snatching up the hook, then hiding it in a bracken of low, squat pines.

Dr. Lassiter Kulley—no one knew his real name, except perhaps the KGB. He was the spymaster, Martin—or Vassily Vocienkov—his trigger man. When Lassiter Kulley made one of his innumerable televised sermons, he actually spoke in code, telling Soviet operatives around the United States and Canada their assignments, using books of the Bible as code references, then specific passages as more detailed operation orders. CIA had monitored him for years. But it had been only during the last two years that Kulley had undertaken his most daring initiative. The kidnapping of American scientists from American soil; once again he used his sermons to coordinate the actual operations, under the unwitting cover of a group of satanic blood cultists. He had traded his leadership and a free flow of victims for their aid. It was the most bizarre cover any agent had ever used, Costigan had said. And because it was, it worked.

Costigan had said nothing about monitoring the cover, or about allowing the deaths of countless hitchhikers and runaways over the past two years. That had all been done in the name of getting concrete proof, catching Kulley in the act—and at the same time channeling a man into the KGB pipeline. The black agriscientist kidnapped slightly more than two months earlier—an agent of the CIA, his mission a convoluted one, to subtly redirect the Soviet agriresearch away from the means of achieving its goal.

And into it all—the deception, the murder, the espionage game—first Frost and Bess, then Mike O'Hara had fallen. And now O'Hara was the only impediment to putting the lid on Kulley.

Frost started out of the pine bracken, across the manicured lawn, toward the brilliantly lit house.

But he didn't run. According to Costigan again, there were photoelectric eyes which automatically triggered television monitor pickup on the security panel in the guard room. Frost stopped, freezing, seeing one of the photoelectric eye units. It was located at chest height, and beneath it at approximately mid-shin level, another unit. He followed the course of the beam with his eye, about fifteen yards away, the matching sensors were positioned in what appeared otherwise to be a normal tree stump.

Frost ducked, raising his left leg over the path of the lower beam, keeping his head and shoulders tucked down beneath the upper beam. He pulled his right leg after him, started to turn, then stopped. There was a third beam, this at abdomen height and perhaps eighteen inches beyond the previous beams—he was less than an inch away from it. Holding his breath, trying to drop as straight as he could, he fell to his knees, crawling under the beam.

Past it, he stopped, catching his breath. There was a laser scan setup farther ahead, and without cumbersome equipment, he couldn't bypass it. But there was another way around it, one he had decided upon when Costigan had shown him the aerial photos of the estate, the architectural plans of the house. The guard room in the basement. It was the only portion of the house other than the front door that was not guarded by a laser scan. The front door would be impenetrable, but where else could one expect to be safer than in a guard room?

Mentally recalling the layout, he started toward it. The KG-99 swung around in front of his body now, his right fist on the pistol grip, his left fist curled

175

around the ventilated barrel shroud just forward of the magazine well, just behind the flash deflector. The gun's safety was off.

There was a flagstone pathway leading to the guard station. Frost crossed over, then under another net of photoelectric eyes, before he started down the path.

On either side of him, there were photoelectric eyes to warn against anyone who strayed from the path; the thought of Kulley straying from "the path" amused him. And though he couldn't see them, he knew that laser sensing devices flanked the path as well.

There had been one more thing Costigan had told him, one small thing about Kulley. Opinions of agency psychiatrists were that Kulley had become so involved in the satanic cult that it had come to be of greater importance to him than his mission for KGB, that it had become an obsession with him—that Kulley was insane.

Frost stopped, halfway down the path toward the guard station, hearing footsteps ahead of him.

The one-eyed man had nowhere to go. Another version of the story of his life. He smiled. He stood motionless, the moonlight bathing the path, instinctively clutching the KG-99 more tightly.

The figure was that of a man, and in an instant Frost realized the figure—a sentry or security man?—would spot him, raise an alarm. Frost thought that perhaps he should have accepted Costigan's offer of a silenced pistol. But involuntarily now, he shook his head. This one would be his own way.

The figure stopped, the silhouette of an assault rifle against its side.

Frost cleared his throat. "Hi. I'm the man from the CIA. I'm here to kill you."

The one-eyed man snapped the KG-99's trigger three times, the shots so loud they sounded in the still-

176

ness like someone playing a Sousa march in a bath-room. The figure doubled over and fell.

Frost started to run—toward the guard room.

Chapter Twenty-One

It was like a ballet that your mind choreographed; you became so good at killing over the years. You dodged right, dodged left, dropped to your knees, did a roll, fired, snapped the muzzle around to a fresh target and fired again. An anonymous body gave up on the gunplay and hurtled at you. You fired at it. Then another tried and the heel of your left hand smashed up under the nose, driving it into the brain. You watched all this as an outside observer.

The one-eyed man stood there, by the door of the guard room, six men dead.

He started inside, toward the light.

He changed sticks in the KG-99. The Interdynamics 9mm, along with his High Power, his knife and his watch had been all that had been found at the estate owned by the dummy corporation. Why they had been left after he and Bess had escaped, he had not comprehended. Only the watch had had sentimental value, the guns and the knife being replaceable. And Bess's clothes had been there, too, as if after he had been knocked unconscious, he and Bess had been taken away and his weapons taken in case there was a use for them. The little Model 36 Bess had illegally borrowed from the dead Mary Boles had never turned up. Likely one of the security people or one of the Satanists had taken it as a souvenir; it had sported ivory grips.

As Frost kicked through the door into the guard room, firing a long semiauto burst from the KG-99 into two more of the security men, he found the little revolver. It was in the hand of the man riding the security monitoring consoles. As he turned to fire it, Frost put three slugs into his forehead.

The one-eyed man left the gun and the man who'd stolen it where they lay.

He stood there, the flash-deflector/compensator unit of the KG-99 slightly hot to his touch as he checked its firmness against the muzzle, his eye scanning the television monitors.

"Shit!" he murmured. There was no panic in the halls; the house and the grounds were empty.

Hearing the sounds of helicopters in the distance, he lowered the muzzle of his weapon. The FBI and Costigan, the CIA "liaison officer" or in plain English, the controller.

There was a desk opposite the security monitoring console and Frost walked toward it. Only one of the drawers was locked. He raised the KG-99, stepped back, and pumped a 115-grain JHP into the lock. The bullet whined as it ricocheted away, burying itself in the acoustical-tiled low ceiling. Frost reached for the drawer, the metal around the lock hot to his touch. He wrenched it open. What he saw inside made his heart sink.

There was a shoulder holster and a Cobra ankle holster. Frost set down the KG-99, taking up the ankle holster. There was a stainless Model 60 Chiefs' Special in it. He opened the cylinder; the gun was fully loaded.

He picked up the shoulder rig, extracting the revolver from it. Pachmayr-gripped, Mag-Na-Ported, Metalifed, the corners of the rear sight blade rounded . . . He opened the cylinder, noting two indented primers, two rounds fired. It was O'Hara's Smith & Wesson Model 29. Only two of the .44 Mag rounds had been used and Frost hoped O'Hara had connected with them. "Mike," he rasped, ramming the revolver back into the shoulder rig and dropping it down on the desk.

Kulley had O'Hara—and O'Hara wasn't the type to have given up his guns.

Frost hammered his fist down on the desk top as Costigan and Cummins came into the guard room.

"Looks like they vacated," Costigan observed.

"Hell of a good security job you guys did," Frost snapped. He pulled the black bandanna down from his mouth and lit a cigarette.

"Whose guns are those?" Cummins asked.

"Mike O'Hara's guns."

"I'll take—"

Frost's right hand closed down over Costigan's wrist as the CIA man reached for the guns. "I'll take them," Frost said evenly. "If O'Hara's alive, when I find him he'll need them. And if he isn't, I'll ram 'em up your butt."

Chapter Twenty-Two

Frost sat in the leather-padded armchair, listening to Costigan and Cummins—Costigan saying, "Evidently their latest kidnap victim will be their last."

"Who?" Frost asked.

"Dr. Erwin Snell—a microbiologist." Cummins looked at Costigan as if wondering in retrospect if it had been all right to say it.

"What," Frost began, lighting a cigarette, "does a microbiologist have to do with a bunch of agriscientists—or am I—"

"No. I may as well tell you. If you get killed, it won't matter, and if you don't, you won't talk about it after we pay you. What do you know about nuclear weapons?"

"I don't like them too much." Frost smiled back.

"Most people don't. But the problem is what do you do to bring the enemy to his knees if needed? If you don't want to risk blowing up the world or any of the other thousand or so hypotheses for the aftermath of a nuclear exchange."

"Gee, I don't know, Costigan. What?"

"Biological warfare—but aimed only at the enemy's breadbasket." Costigan cleared his throat, then added, "Only as a last resort, of course."

"You guys were working on something to destroy Soviet crops—to—"

"A microorganism—once applied to an area it

spreads like wildfire through the air, but it evolves as it regenerates, after approximately ten days evolving into a harmless organism that becomes sterile. It's perfect. Plunk it into the middle of Russia—not literally of course—and whammo—nothing grows that year—not even a tree. But by the time it crosses into western Europe, the organism has evolved into something totally harmless which cannot reproduce and eventually dies. Perfect!''

"That's why you didn't tell O'Hara to watch out for Kulley?" Frost murmured.

"Exactly—I'm glad to see you understand. Once the Russians had our agriteam, well, they had to know what we were working on. So, they'd want the microbiologist—Dr. Snell. Well, we fed them our man, to take them off in the wrong research direction; they guarded Dr. Snell more closely than we guard the president."

"Well . . ." Frost smiled. "We all know how well that can work." Cummins visibly bristled at the remark, but said nothing. "But they got Snell anyway?"

"Uh-huh." Costigan nodded. "He went to his daughter's dance recital, had to use the bathroom. Just like something out of a movie. The recital hall had been rigged. Snell walked into one of the stalls—the only one not out of order—"

"You should have known better." Frost nodded.

"Agreed—but it was the FBI, not us." Costigan smiled again.

Cummins said nothing.

"Anyway," Costigan went on. "Just like a movie. The FBI agent waited outside the stall, but as the stall door closed, the entire stall was pulled back into the wall and a steel door slammed down across the opening in the wall. The agent ran into the hallway, hammered down the door into the next room—a storage

182

room—and was shot to death. But before he died, he said he saw Snell, unconscious, being stuffed into a box. What happened after that, we don't know."

"Why did—?"

"The restaurant where he'd eaten the night of the recital—his favorite place to take his daughter and we couldn't talk him out of it. Fifty-seven persons who ate there that night came down with a mild case of food poisoning, all of them reporting loose bowels."

"What a chump play." Frost coughed through a cloud of cigarette smoke.

"Unfortunately, we were the chumps." Costigan smiled again.

"We feel," Cummins said, "that Kulley has some secret route out of the country, and that he is planning to evacuate along with his prisoner—or prisoners, if O'Hara is still alive."

"Clever of you to figure that out." Frost nodded.

"Captain Frost, I'm just trying to outline—"

"I know." Frost nodded. "I'm just in a lousy mood."

"I appreciate the friendship between yourself and Agent O'Hara, and the help you've given this agency in the past—"

"Wholly unintentional."

"Damn it." Cummins rose from his chair, his pinkish fists balled and shaking. "I want Mike O'Hara to get out of this alive, too!"

"Gentlemen," Costigan said loudly, "we won't get—"

"Anywhere with this," Frost interrupted. "So fine—what's the plan?"

"All right," Cummins said, pacing the room now as he talked, hands behind him like an admiral. "All right. The sermons were always the key—right? So, the last sermon we very carefully analyzed and we fi-

183

nally broke the code—too late, but we broke it anyway. He was calling for a rally to—what the—" He searched his pockets, extracting a small note pad from the left inside breast pocket, then flipping through it. "He called for something to do with the—"

Cummins stopped, turning his head toward the doorway. Bess was coming through into the sitting room beside a uniformed Atlanta policeman. "Miss Stallman." Costigan nodded. "What—?"

"I had Cummins call her," Frost told him, standing then walking over to Bess and taking her in his arms. He planted a quick kiss on her lips, heard her murmur something in his ear, then turned and faced Costigan. "I figured if we were doing a skull session, she's the closest thing to a resident expert on Satanists. She was doing enough research with Mary Boles before Mary was murdered, and if Kulley is as cracked as you say he is, he's probably got something involved with the satanic cult in his escape plan."

"I don't know if you could call me an expert," she smiled. "In fact, I'm not an expert. I've read a lot about it—or did before—"

"Try this then," Cummins said, turning back to his notebook. "What would a recurring reference to the Passover have to do with a satanic cult?"

"Nothing," she shrugged. "I mean—I'm Jewish. I can tell you all about the Passover celebration, about its origins—whatever—but—" She stopped, looking out the sitting-room window across the grounds, Frost a few feet behind her. He started toward her, staring out across the grounds.

She looked up at him, then murmured, "the full moon—Passover is celebrated—"

"Full moon," Costigan repeated.

"There's a full moon tonight," Bess murmured.

Frost looked at his Rolex—it was fourteen minutes

184

to eleven. "Midnight and full moons—it's tonight. He's leaving tonight." Frost glanced at the Rolex again. "In just seventy-four minutes."

Chapter Twenty-Three

If a full moon was the criterion, and the estate where Frost and Bess had been held with its "inside" demonic shrine would be too hot—on that Frost, Bess, Cummins, and Costigan had found themselves in total agreement—the satanic cult service would be held out-of-doors, in a wooded area, but somewhere suitable for a small plane to land.

For suddenly, the entire scheme of things had fallen into place. Cummins had called the man in charge of fire prevention for the Georgia Department of Forestry, rousted him from bed to ask of reported remains of bonfires in northern Georgia over the last two years. The man had thought Cummins was insane, as Cummins had told it, but after a little prompting had agreed to make some calls and check. While waiting for the word on bonfire traces, with the help of Atlanta P.D. a map had been made showing the approximate locations of the mutilation murders possibly attributable to satanic cultists. Six bodies had been found over the course of nineteen months.

Having plotted those locations, then with the return call from the forestry official, having plotted the locations of bonfire remains, they had a specific geographic area.

Frost stood before the map, studying it. "The mountains—almost near the Carolina border," Frost murmured. "We need one other thing—maybe Civil

Air Patrol, the air force—maybe the marine corps—I've seen Harriers do low-to-the-ground afterburner flights around here. We need to find out where in this area a small plane could land," he told Cummins and Costigan. Then he looked at the Rolex again. "And we need to know in forty-three minutes or less. You got that plane on tap?"

"Helicopter outside to take you to the airfield ten miles from here, and the plane will start preflighting the moment I call," Cummins said.

"Have him preflight now—then you radio me aboard the plane and give me the tightest area you can work up. We'll look for signs of a bonfire and I'll bail out. Once I've got Martin in sight and Kulley, too, I'll activate the signal. You come in with the choppers and fast."

"Agreed." Costigan nodded. He picked up the cigarette lighter–sized gadget and handed it to Frost. "Now—these things don't work as good as they say they do in the movies. Flip this toggle switch, then hit this button. It'll emit a high-frequency signal we can pick up and home in on. But don't hit it prematurely. It'll go for five minutes before the batteries wear down—and that's it."

Frost turned it over in his right hand. "Doesn't have one hundred eighty-six different deadly functions?"

"Just a homing device. Any dogs around, it'll drive 'em wacko—ultrahigh frequency."

"Wonderful," Frost murmured. He dropped the thing into his pocket, walked out toward the doors, and stooped to kiss Bess—once, hard, and long. She started to speak, but he told her, "I know," then walked through the doorway into the hall. Already, he could faintly hear the sound of the helicopter rotors outside. . . .

He hadn't bailed out of an airplane in a long time. It

wasn't something he'd missed much either; it was dangerous work at night, over unfamiliar territory heavily forested. They had spotted the bonfire five minutes earlier, but from a distance—he hoped distance enough that the noise of the single-engine Beachcraft had not attracted attention on the ground.

He had checked his weapons, that the chamber of the KG-99 was clear, that all three spare magazines were loaded full; that gave him a gross of 9mm 115-grain JHPs to throw, counting the magazine in the weapon. He had dropped the magazine from the Metalifed High Power, cleared the chamber in the event of jump impact. Then he loaded the chambered round back into the magazine, shoved the magazine back up the well, and reholstered the gun in the Cobra rig. He had checked the chute, but it had been prepacked. He absently hoped the packer had known what he or she had been doing.

He gave an extra tug to the KG-99's sling, to keep the assault pistol close across his chest. In a knapsack under his left arm he carried O'Hara's big .44 Magnum and the loaded speedloaders with the 180-grain JHPs O'Hara liked. He'd left the shoulder rig and the little ankle gun behind. If O'Hara needed extra armament, Frost would have created enough of a surplus just getting to him.

The pilot had his dome light lit, and was giving Frost a thumbs-up signal as Frost turned back to look at him.

The one-eyed man grunted, saying, "I know; you wish you could do this." Frost worked the passenger-door handle, then pushed the door out against the slipstream, carefully stepping out onto the wing stem. The wind was high, rocking the wing under him slightly as he prepared to jump. He looked skyward—the full moon—then at his Rolex. It was two minutes

188

before midnight.

The one-eyed man pushed himself off, hurtling down into the darkness, spreading his arms and legs as though he could fly, to slow and to control his descent. He wanted to hold off on pulling the ripcord until the last possible moment, to guide himself toward a gentle piece of ground if he could find one, and at the same time get as close as possible to the open field where the bonfire was lit; there wasn't time for a long hike.

He watched the altimeter strapped to the auxiliary chute pack across his chest, watched the needle as it danced, ever downward. He could see little of the landscape below him despite the full moon, but when the altimeter reached what he gauged as the minimum safe height, he pulled the ripcord for his primary chute; he hadn't allowed enough time to use the auxiliary chute if necessary. There was a jerk, wrenching at his shoulders and back, and his chute was open above him, the chute black like the clothes he wore, like the fingerless gloves over his hands, like the ninja-style scarf that covered his hair and the one that covered his face. He tugged at the guidelines, trying for a small clearing to the south, the wind battering him northward. He jerked again at the guidelines. The chute finally drifted toward the edge of the small clearing.

He felt something brush at his legs, then a heavy thudding against his thighs, then an abrupt jerk.

"Damn it," he rasped. He was hung in a tree.

He couldn't properly gauge the distance to the ground, but he made it roughly twenty feet.

He reached under the chute pack to his Gerber Mk-I knife. "Here goes nothin'," he rasped, beginning to hack away the guidelines for the chute. He cut the last one, then dropped, electing to hold onto the knife lest he lose it in darkness.

He hit the ground hard, rolled, and stopped, his left

189

ankle hurting a little, his right elbow hurting a lot—a rock.

He could move the arm, though he realized it'd be stiff in the morning—if there was a morning. He'd hurt his elbow years earlier while on leave in Japan, and ever after that had referred to the injury as "Ping-Pong elbow."

He tried standing up, and found that his ankle worked.

Holstering the knife, he reached out the covered lensatic compass and took a quick bearing, nodding to himself that it had confirmed what he had already mentally determined as the proper direction. He pocketed the compass, worked the bolt and then the safety on the KG-99, then chambered a round into the High Power. He reholstered the High Power, leaving its hammer down. He readjusted the sling of the KG-99, getting the gun down from his chest to belt level, so he could use the sling to steady the assault pistol when he fired.

Holding the pistol grip of the KG-99 in his right fist, he took off at a long-strided commando walk across the clearing. A glance at the Rolex made it five after midnight—the service would be under way. . . .

The one-eyed man could see what Cummins and Costigan had meant; Kulley had really gone over, Satanism his obsession now rather than the KGB. Even without a knowledge of cultism, Frost could tell that the ceremony he watched was one of great elaborateness. Kulley wore the same satin robe he had worn weeks earlier, the robe raised now as a body-painted nude dancer first kissed his feet, then moved her hands lovingly up his legs to kiss his behind. But this time, no sacrifice was yet on the altar, not even an altar—just a massive rock that looked from where Frost observed to have been hauled there.

190

The body-painted dancer climbed atop the makeshift altar, two naked men helping her, then she lay down across it, face down.

Candles—black as far as Frost could make out—were placed in each of her hands, then lit from a torch taken from the bonfire at the center of the circle of naked worshipers surrounding it and the altar.

Frost snugged up against the tree trunk more closely, wary of his perch some fifteen feet above the ground. He had seen Kulley—that much of the mission was complete—but now he needed to see Martin. Then he could blow the whistle—activiate the homing device and hopefully Costigan, Cummins, and the troops would show up. But the plane was necessary, too; it had to land, to pick up Dr. Snell, the microbiologist.

There was loud chanting, but in English, the chant the most creative combination of obscenities Frost had ever heard—in fact some of the words new to him, he realized. At one phrase, unconsciously he murmured, "Two people can't do that—impossible."

A new phase of the service had begun. A robed figure, walking dumbly, was being brought out of the shadows at the edge of the clearing; two black-robed figures aided the white-robed figure in the center. Frost decided it was a woman—the one in white. A virgin?

The woman was led toward the human altar made by the body-painted woman, the black candles flickering in the now-slight wind. The white robe was stripped from the head and upper body of the woman. From the size of her breasts, Frost determined she was perhaps fourteen—and obviously drugged from the way in which she moved.

The woman was brought closer to the altar as Kulley raised the ritual killing sword. "Holy shit," Frost

191

murmured. He started to shinny down the tree trunk toward the ground.

As he reached the ground, he could just make out the girl being placed upon the human altar, face up, buttocks to buttocks with the body-painted woman. The chanting increased, and the circle of naked Satanists began a wild dancing that Frost, almost spellbound for an instant, watched. He guessed it was an orgy, for the men and women—and sometimes couples of the same sex—were performing sexual acts with each other as they danced. "Not easy to do," he murmured, then started away from the trees.

Had the Satanists been robed, he would have nailed one of them, donned the robe and worked his way closer to the altar. But life wasn't like that for him, he decided—easy.

Frost edged the perimeter of the clearing, to get as close to the altar as possible. Despite the fact that he hadn't seen Martin, or any sign of an airplane, or any sign of O'Hara, he couldn't risk letting the teen-age girl on the altar be killed.

The dancers' bodies glistened in the light of the bonfire as they kept up their chants of obscenities, their copulation, Kulley dipping the killing sword into ram's blood and painting the young girl's body with it.

Frost had reached the edge of the clearing nearest to the altar, the place from which the young girl had been brought. The two black-robed men who had escorted her were there, waiting.

Frost unslung the KG-99, then started toward the nearest one; the second man was obsessed with watching the dancing, the ritual. Frost moved slowly, the noise of the chanting and screaming covering the sound of his footfalls.

He stopped, less than a yard behind the robed man. The one-eyed man slung the sling from the KG-99 up and over and down, around the man's throat, then he wheeled, jerking on it, snapping the man over his shoulder, the sound of the neck breaking a loud crack.

Frost crouched, wheeling and waiting for the second man to have heard him. But there was no movement.

Frost dragged the body across the ground, toward a clump of bushes, then quickly stripped away the black robe. Life was getting easier, he decided. . . .

The robe covered him to the ankles, its hooded portion low over his face with the KG-99 slung under it, the High Power in his right hand covered by the folds of the left sleeve. Monklike, head lowered, he walked toward the second robed man, waiting, saying nothing.

His mouth open as he chanted, Kulley was raising the killing sword, blood dripping from it.

Frost glanced left—the black robed man beside him was watching Kulley. Frost took the High Power from the fold of his left sleeve and using his left fist, smashed it down butt-first against the right rear portion of the robed man's skull. He thought he heard a slight crunching sound as the body fell.

Frost walked in front of it, replacing the pistol, and by standing there, blocking the body from view.

The dancing had stopped, the glistening bodies forming up again into a ragged circle around the human altar and the human sacrifice resting upon it.

The one-eyed man had killed five guards on the way toward the clearing, and he assumed that was the bulk of the security. So if he could get the girl free, all he'd have to worry about would be the three or four dozen people in the clearing, all of them now picking up their knives. He shrugged. There were more than a dozen cars parked a half-mile down from the clearing, and Georgians were notoriously bad about locking cars and taking keys. The one-eyed man smiled—considering that everyone except Kulley and the two men Frost himself had just killed was stark naked, there really wasn't anyplace they could have put their keys.

He could make it with the drugged girl to one of the cars, maybe shoot out some tires and then drive like hell. He could drop the girl, then double back and look for O'Hara. He saw a torchlight at the far end of the clearing, a good distance away since the clearing was longer than it was wide, vastly so. Then, shortly after seeing the first light, he saw another, then another, then another—"Beacons," he rasped.

And now, the chanting momentarily stopped as Kulley raised the sword again, Frost could hear the sound of an aircraft engine.

Kulley raved about homage to Satin, sacrifice, the blood of the ram. "Crap," Frost muttered.

From the far edge of the clearing opposite him, Frost now saw a procession, torchlit, of robed figures starting from the trees.

Only the first two and last two in the procession carried torches; the two in the center were robed like the others, but with their hands behind them. He recognized the long loping shuffle of the second of the two torchless figures—O'Hara.

Frost's right fist balled on the butt of the High Power. One of the four torchbearers would be Martin. He felt it inside him.

He could see aircraft running lights, low on the far horizon now, but growing brighter. When the aircraft landed, Kulley would kill the sacrificial virgin—to the delight of his followers and to their distraction. It could have been drugs coming in on the plane, or illegal aliens or anything—they wouldn't care. Drugs were probably part of what they did, why they danced, Frost guessed. Either that or they were all in-

194

sane. "Devil-worshipers," he murmured. The thought amused him. He was someone the world labeled a "bad guy," a mercenary, and he stood there alone, ready to challenge a priest of the devil and the KGB to save a girl he didn't know and probably wouldn't have liked, an FBI agent, and a microbiologist who was plotting bacteriological warfare against the Soviet Union. He decided life didn't make sense.

The timing would be critical. He alternately watched the procession of torchbearers as it moved toward the far end of the field, the growing landing lights, and Kulley's killing sword as it wavered over the ram's blood–painted body of the sacrificial victim on the human altar.

If he had read it in a book, he would have thought it impossible, he decided, crazy. But it was happening to him.

He decided also it was likely he'd die—the odds were a little heavy.

The plane was taxiing in now and as Frost glanced toward the procession of torchbearers, he saw the figure he'd picked as O'Hara lash out with his foot, nudge against the second torchless figure, then start to run, the second figure behind him.

"Ha ha!" The one-eyed man started toward the altar, the Metalifed High Power in his right fist, raised high in the air. He was running, lifting the bottom of the black robe he wore like a woman would lift her skirt. He shouted, "Kulley!"

The priest of Satan, his hands dripping blood like his killing sword, turned, the light of the bonfire making his sweating face seem to glow.

Frost aimed the High Power, then fired twice, Kulley's smile gone, his face gone as the 115-grain JHPs impacted into it.

Frost jumped to the altar, pressing the muzzle of the

High Power against the head of the woman who was the living altar. She wasn't living anymore when he pulled the trigger, once, then once again. With his left hand he grabbed the girl, dragging her from the corpse under her, the pistol bucking in his hands again as he started with her from the altar, naked Satanists falling to the ground, their knives flailing, cutting the air around him. The one-eyed man pushed the girl ahead of him into the trees, stripping the robe as he ran, then ramming the cocked and locked High Power into his belt, swinging the KG-99 around into a firing position, wheeling. He offed the safety, then started to press the trigger.

Naked, sweating bodies fell before him in waves. He could hear the "virgin" he'd rescued screaming as he kept up shooting.

The pistol was empty, and he rammed a fresh magazine home, stuffing the empty into his belt; then he grabbed the girl by the hand and started to run again along the edge of the open field, toward where O'Hara and the second man were heading—the treeline opposite the twin-engine plane which had landed.

Frost could hear the engines revving, see the plane start taxiing to get itself turned around and into the wind.

Gunfire—from one of the robed figures chasing O'Hara and the second figure.

The shooter was seventy-five yards away. Frost raised the KG-99, steadying it against the side of a tree, mentally crossing his fingers as he pumped the trigger once, twice; then on the third round, the gunfire from the field ceased.

The body fell; Frost grabbed the girl and started to run again.

"Mike! Mike!"

Frost shouted as he ran, breathless. More of the Sa-

196

tanists were coming into the woods after him, knives and swords in their hands.

He struck out of the tree line, into the field, running toward O'Hara.

The man behind O'Hara stumbled and fell; O'Hara stopped. A man was running up toward O'Hara, a torch in his left hand, a pistol in his right. O'Hara turned toward the man, hands still locked behind his back—Frost guessed tied or cuffed.

Frost stopped running, dropping to his knees, shouting, "Mike—hit the dirt!"

O'Hara dropped; Frost fired over him, the KG-99 bucking in his hands, making thudding sounds as the action worked so close to his face as he fired. The man with the pistol fell.

Frost pushed himself to his feet, grabbing the naked girl again and running. O'Hara ran toward him.

"Untie me!"

"Do this, do that," Frost snapped. O'Hara turned his back to him. Frost grabbed at the Gerber, hacking the ropes across O'Hara's wrists; then as O'Hara started to move his hands, Frost shoved the Metalifed Model 29 into his right fist.

"You're thoughtful, Frost—damned thoughtful," O'Hara shouted, swinging up the big .44 Magnum, aiming it behind Frost's head, and pulling the trigger.

Frost's ears rang. "Thoughtful," O'Hara shouted, "but careless."

Frost wheeled, the KG-99 in an assault position at his hip. A naked dead man holding a sword lay in the grass less than five yards from him.

The one-eyed man rasped, "Thanks—is one of those guys—?"

"Yeah—Vassily Vocienkov of the KGB—shit!"

Frost followed O'Hara's stare—two robed figures ran toward the aircraft which was taxiing fast for posi-

197

tion.

"Keep an eye on the girl. She's spaced out and scared to death," Frost rasped, then threw O'Hara the small knapsack. "Ammo in there—good luck," and Frost started to run.

He suddenly remembered the beeper, the little radio alert that he carried in his trouser pocket. He felt for it as he ran, found it, flipped the toggle switch, then depressed the button. He dropped it back into his pocket, kept running.

The plane was into a takeoff position now, perhaps a hundred yards ahead of him and to his left. Frost started firing the KG-99 as he ran, gunfire coming back to him from the two men running toward the plane.

"Martin!" Frost shouted the word like a curse, so loud his throat ached with it.

The KG-99 was empty and Frost dropped it on its sling, letting it hang across his back as he leaned into the run, the High Power now in his right fist, more than half-empty, he knew.

One of the two robed figures was beside the plane. Frost flopped to his knees, the pistol extended ahead of him in both fists. He pumped the trigger once, then once more, the slide locking open, empty. "Shit!" But the man beside the aircraft fell.

Frost pushed himself to his feet, dropping the High Power to the ground, swinging the KG-99 back, dumping the empty magazine, letting it drop to the ground, fumbling a full spare from his belt, ramming it up the well, then running on.

The last one had to be him—"Martin!"

The plane was moving now, the last robed figure racing toward it, jumping for the wing stem, going for the door on the passenger side.

Frost swung the KG-99 into an assault position, firing at the plane as he ran, his bullets ripping into the fuselage. The plane moved faster now, faster, the robed figure struggling to open the passenger door.

Frost zigzagged, changing direction to run toward the plane, up alongside it, depressing the KG-99's safety as he jumped, his hands grabbing at the robed figure.

The prop draft blew away the hood of the robe as the man on the wing stem turned toward him, hands going for the one-eyed man's throat.

"Martin!" Frost's left fist hammered out. The one-eyed man lost his balance, lurched forward as his fist slammed hard against the middle of the assassin's face.

Martin lurched back, his hands reaching out across the nose of the fuselage, his hands slipping, his body slipping—into the propeller blades.

Frost's face and hands were sprayed with blood and bits of flesh. A hideous scream started but never finished; body parts flashed skyward toward the moonlight like a fireworks display.

The aircraft under Frost was starting to take off. The one-eyed man, the man they called a mercenary, rammed the barrel of the KG-99 forward with his free right hand, his left hand balancing him beside the passenger door. The flash-deflector/recoil-compensator unit at the muzzle of the assault pistol punctured and shattered the glass in the passenger door, Frost's left hand free for an instant to work off the safety. His balance went as he fired, pumping the trigger again and again and again into the face of the KGB pilot at the small plane's controls.

Frost toppled back, thudding hard against the ground. The rear wings of the aircraft brushed over him, just missing his head. The aircraft started up, then pitched forward, onto its nose, its fuselage exploding as the plane cartwheeled end over end into the trees.

In the distance, the roar of the explosions still coming from the plane almost drowning out the sound, Frost could hear the whirring of rotor blades in the night, as he'd heard so many times before on battlefields in Vietnam, in Latin America, in the Middle East and Africa.

He pushed himself to his feet, for once in his life unscathed.

He snatched the black bandanna from his hair, using it to wipe the blood away from his face. He dropped it to the ground, pulling free the second one from around his neck.

The fingerless cloth gloves were saturated with blood. He pulled them off, dropping them into the shadow near his feet.

Orange light flickered across the field now, from the burning plane; and in the light, he could see a robed figure approaching him, but in its right hand was a familiar object—the big .44 revolver. It was O'Hara, the hood of the robe pushed down.

He stopped less than a yard away from Frost and transferred the revolver to his left hand. The first of the FBI helicopters was landing now. O'Hara extended his hand, his voice low, saying, "Thanks—for savin' my bacon, Hank."

Frost took the hand. "I'd say anytime, but I don't think I wanna do this again for a while, Mike."

His hands shaking a little, the assault pistol slung at his side, the one-eyed man found his battered Zippo, and rolling the striking wheel under his bloodstained thumb, poked the tip of a bent-out-of-shape Camel into the flickering blue-yellow flame.

He inhaled hard. O'Hara alive, Martin and the hypocritical Kulley both dead.

The one-eyed man exhaled a cloud of gray smoke into the moonlight. And at "home," Bess waited—for him, Hank Frost.